A CHRISTMAS JOURNEY

A CHRISTMAS JOURNEY

Anne Perry

headline

First published in Great Britain in 2003
by HEADLINE BOOK PUBLISHING

10 9 8 7 6 5 4 3 2 1

Cataloguing in Publication Data is available
from the British Library

ISBN 0 7553 2114 6

Typeset in Times New Roman by
Letterpart Limited, Reigate, Surrey

Printed and bound in Great Britain by
Mackays of Chatham plc, Chatham, Kent

HEADLINE BOOK PUBLISHING
A division of Hodder Headline
338 Euston Road
LONDON NW1 3BH

www.headline.co.uk
www.hodderheadline.com

A CHRISTMAS JOURNEY

A Christmas Journey
(1st Part)

Lady Vespasia Cumming-Gould hesitated a moment at the top of the stairs. Applecross, in Berkshire was one of those magnificent country houses where one descended down a long curved sweep of marble into the vast hall, where now the assembled guests were gathered, awaiting the call to dinner.

First one person, then another looked up. To wait for them all would have been ostentatious. Vespasia was dressed in oyster satin, not a shade everyone could wear, but Prince Albert himself had said that she was the most beautiful woman in Europe, with her glorious hair and exquisite bones. It was not a remark that had endeared her to the Queen, the more so since it was probably true.

But this was not a royal occasion; it was a simple weekend party early in December. The London Season, with its hectic social round, was over, and those who had country homes had returned to them to look forward to Christmas. There were rumours of possible war in the Crimea, but apart from that the middle of the century saw only greater progress and prosperity within an empire that spanned the globe.

Omegus Jones came to the foot of the stairs to meet his guest. He was not only the perfect host, but also a friend of some years, even though he was in his fifties, and Vespasia was barely past thirty. Her husband, older than she, was the one who had first made the acquaintance. Her children were in the house in London, safe and well cared for.

'My dear Vespasia, you are quite ravishing,' Omegus said with a self-deprecating smile. 'Of which you cannot fail to be aware, so please do not insult my intelligence by pretending surprise, or worse still, denial.' He was a lean man with a wry face, full of humour, and an unconscious elegance as much at home in a country lane as a London withdrawing room.

'Thank you,' she accepted. A witty reply would have been inappropriate, and anyway, his candour had robbed her of the ability to think of one.

There were a dozen people here, including herself. The most socially prominent were Lord and Lady Salchester, closely followed by Sir John and Lady Warburton. Lady Warburton's sister had married a duke, as she found a dozen ways of reminding people. Actually Vespasia's father had been an earl, but she never spoke of it. It was birth, not achievement, and those who mattered already knew. To remind people was indelicate, as if you had no other worth to yourself, never mind to them.

Also present were Fenton and Blanche Twyford, two eminently eligible young men, Peter Hanning and Bertie Rosythe, Gwendolen Kilmuir, widowed over a year ago, and Isobel Alvie, who had lost her husband nearly three years ago now.

It was not customary to serve refreshments before dinner, simply to converse until the butler should sound the gong. The guests would then go into the dining room in strict order of precedence, the rules for which were intricate and must never be broken.

Lady Salchester, a formidable horsewoman, was dressed in a deep wine shade, with a crinoline skirt of daunting proportions. She was speaking of last season's races, in particular the meeting at Royal Ascot.

'Magnificent creature!' she said enthusiastically, her voice booming a little. 'Nothing else stood a chance.'

Lady Warburton smiled as if in agreement.

Bertie Rosythe, slender, fair, superbly tailored, was trying to mask his boredom, and doing it rather well. If Vespasia had not known him, she might have been duped into imagining he was interested.

Isobel was beside her, darkly striking, less than beautiful, but with fine eyes, and a ready wit.

'Magnificent creature indeed,' she whispered. 'And Lady Salchester herself certainly never had a chance.'

'What are you talking about?' Vespasia asked, knowing that there must be many layers to the remark.

'Fanny Oakley,' Isobel replied, leaning even closer. 'Didn't you see her at Ascot? Whatever were you doing?'

'Watching the horses,' Vespasia answered drily.

'Don't be absurd!' Isobel laughed. 'Good heavens! You didn't have money on them, did you? I mean real money?'

Vespasia saw by her face that she was suddenly concerned in case Vespasia were in gambling debt, not an unheard-of difficulty for a young woman of considerable means and very little to occupy herself, her husband away a good deal of the time and endless staff to care for her home and her children.

Vespasia wondered for a chill moment if Isobel were really acute enough in her observation to have seen the vague, sad stirrings of emptiness in Vespasia's marriage, and at least half to have understood them. One wished to have friends – without them life would hold only shallow pleasures – but there were areas of the heart into which one did not intrude. Some aches could be borne only in secret. Isobel could not have guessed what had happened in Rome during the passionate revolutions of '48. No one could. That was a once-in-a-lifetime love, to be buried now and thought of only in dreams. She and Mario Corena would not meet again. This here in Applecross was the world of reality.

'Not at all,' Vespasia replied lightly. 'The race does not need the edge of money to make it fun.'

'Are you referring to the horses?' Isobel asked softly.

'What else?' Vespasia retorted.

Isobel laughed.

Lord Salchester saw Vespasia and acknowledged her appreciatively. Lady Salchester smiled with warm lips and a glacial eye.

'Good evening, Lady Vespasia,' she said with penetrating clarity. 'How charming to see you. You seem quite recovered from the exertion of the Season.' It was a less-than-kind reference to a summer cold that had made Vespasia tired and far from herself at the Henley Regatta. 'Let us hope next year is not too strenuous for you,' she added. She was twenty years older than Vespasia, but a woman of immense stamina, who had never been beautiful.

Vespasia was aware of Lord Salchester's eye on her, and even more of Omegus Jones's. It was the latter that tempered her reply. Wit was not always funny if it cut those already wounded. 'I hope so,' she answered. 'It is tedious for everybody when someone cannot keep up. I shall endeavour not to do that again.'

Isobel was surprised. Lady Salchester was astounded.

Vespasia smiled sweetly and excused herself.

Gwendolen Kilmuir was talking earnestly to Bertie Rosythe. Her head was bent a trifle, the light shining on her rich brown hair and the deep plum pink of her gown. She was widowed well over a year now, and had taken the first even remotely possible opportunity to cast aside her black. She was a young woman, barely twenty-eight, and had no intention of spending longer in mourning than Society demanded. She looked up demurely at Bertie, but she was smiling, and her face had a softness and a warmth to it that was hard to mistake.

7

Vespasia glanced at Isobel, and caught a pensive look in her eye. Then she smiled, and it was gone.

Bertie turned and saw them. As always he was gracefully polite. Gwendolen's pleasure was not as easily assumed. Vespasia saw the muscles in her neck and chin tighten and her bosom swell as she breathed deeply before mustering a smile. 'Good evening, Lady Vespasia, Mrs Alvie. How nice it will be to dine together.'

'As always,' Isobel murmured. 'I believe we dined at Lady Cranbourne's also, during the summer? And at the Queen's garden party.' Her eyes flickered up and down Gwendolen's plum taffeta. 'I remember your gown.'

Gwendolen blushed. Bertie smiled uncertainly.

Suddenly, and with a considerable jolt, Vespasia realised that Isobel's interest in Bertie was not as casual as she had supposed. The barb in her remark betrayed her. Such cruelty was not in the character she knew.

'You remember her gown?' she said in feigned surprise. 'How delightful.' She looked with slight disdain at Isobel's russet gold with its sweeping skirts. 'So few gowns are remarkable these days, don't you think?'

Isobel caught her breath, a flare of temper in her eyes.

Gwendolen laughed with a release of tension, and turned to Bertie again.

Lady Warburton joined them and the conversation became enmeshed in gossip, cases of 'he said' and 'she said', and 'do you really believe . . .?'

Dinner was announced, and Omegus Jones offered his arm to Vespasia, which in view of Lady Salchester's presence she found a singular honour, and they went into the long blue and gold dining room in solemn and correct procession, each to his or her appointed place at the glittering table.

The chandeliers were reflected in the gleam of silver, shattered prisms of light on tiers of crystal goblets in a field of linen napkins folded like lilies. The fire burned warm in the grate. White chrysanthemums from the garden filled the bowls on the table, scenting the room with something like earth and autumn leaves, the soft fragrance of woodland.

The dinner began with the lightest consommé. There would be nine courses, but it was not expected that everyone would eat from all of them. Ladies in particular, mindful of the delicate figures and tiny waists demanded by fashion, would choose with care. Where physical survival was relatively easy, one created rules to make social survival more difficult. Not to be accepted was to become an outcast, a person who fitted nowhere.

Conversation turned to more serious topics. Sir John Warburton spoke of the current political situation, giving his views with gravity, his thin hands brown against the white linen of the cloth.

'Do you really think it will come to war?' Peter Hanning asked with a frown.

'With Russia?' Sir John raised his eyebrows. 'It is not impossible.'

'Nonsense!' Lord Salchester said briskly, his wine glass in the air. 'Nobody's going to go to war against us!

Especially over something as absurd as the Crimea! They'll remember Waterloo, and leave us well alone.'

'Waterloo was over thirty-five years ago,' Omegus Jones pointed out. 'The men who fought that have laid their swords by long ago.'

'The British army is still the same, sir!' Salchester retorted, his moustache bristling.

'Indeed, I fear it is,' Omegus agreed quietly, his lips tight, his eyes sad and far away.

'That was the finest, most invincible army in the world,' Salchester's voice grew louder.

'We beat Napoleon,' Omegus corrected. 'But times change. Good and evil do not, nor pride and compassion, but warfare moves all the time – new weapons, new ideas, new strategies.'

'I do not like to disagree with you at your own table, sir,' Salchester responded. 'Courtesy prevents me from telling you what I think of your view.'

Omegus' face lit with a sudden smile, remarkably sweet and quite unaffected. 'Let us hope that nothing happens to prove which one of us is correct.'

Footmen in livery and parlour maids with white lace-trimmed aprons removed the soup plates and served the fish. The butler poured wine. The lights blazed; the clink of silver on porcelain was the soft background as conversation began again.

Vespasia watched rather than listened. Faces, gestures told her more of emotion than the carefully considered words. She saw how often Gwendolen looked towards

Bertie Rosythe, the flush in her face, how easily she laughed when he was amusing, and that it pleased him. He was almost as much aware of her, although he was more careful not to show it quite so openly.

Vespasia was not the only person to notice it. She saw Blanche Twyford's satisfaction, and recalled hearing her make a remark, which now she understood more clearly. She had spoken of spring weddings, and Gwendolen had blushed. Perhaps this was the weekend when a declaration was expected. It would seem so.

Fenton Twyford seemed less pleased by it. His dark face looked cautious. A couple of times his glance at Bertie suggested unease, as if an old shadow crossed his thoughts, but Vespasia had no idea what it might be. Was Bertie not quite as perfectly eligible as he seemed? Or was it Gwendolen who somehow fell short? As far as Vespasia knew, the young widow was of good family, wealthy if undistinguished, and without a breath of scandal attached. Her late husband, Roger Kilmuir, was also blemishless, and connected to the aristocracy. If his far elder brother died childless, which seemed likely, then he would have inherited the title and all that went with it.

Only he had died in an unfortunate accident, the sort of thing that happened occasionally to even the best horsemen. Gwendolen had been quite shattered at the time. It was good to see that she was reaching after some kind of happiness again.

One by one gold-rimmed plates were removed, fresh courses brought, and more wine poured, until there was

11

nothing left but mounds of fresh grapes from the hothouse, and silver finger bowls to remove any faint traces of stickiness.

The ladies excused themselves to the withdrawing room and left the gentlemen to pass the port and, for those who wished to, to smoke.

Vespasia followed Isobel and Lady Salchester, and was aware of the rustle of taffetas and silks as Gwendolen, Lady Warburton and Blanche Twyford came behind them. They took their seats in the velvet-curtained withdrawing room, carefully arranging mountainous skirts to be both flattering and not to impede other people's approach, when the gentlemen should rejoin them.

This was the part of any evening that Vespasia liked the least. Conversation almost always became domestic, and since Rome she found it hard to concentrate on such things. She loved her children – it was deep and instinctive, older than words or the demands of society – and her marriage was agreeable enough. Her husband was kind and intelligent, and an honourable man. Many women would have been envious of so much. She wanted for nothing socially or materially. It was only in the longing of the heart, the hunger to care to the power and depth of her being, that she was not answered.

She looked at the faces of the other women in the room and wondered what lay behind their gracious masks. Lady Salchester had energy and intelligence, but she was plain, plainer than her own parlour maid, and probably the housemaid and the kitchen maid as well. It was widely suspected that Lord Salchester's attention wandered, in a practical as well as imaginary way.

'I know what you are thinking,' Isobel said, beside her, leaning a little closer so she could speak in a whisper.

Vespasia was startled. 'Do you?'

'Of course!' Isobel smiled. 'I was thinking so too. And it is quite unfair. If she were to do the same, with that nice-looking footman, Society would be scandalised, and she would be ruined. She would never go anywhere again!'

'Dozens of married women become bored with their husbands and, after they have produced the appropriate number of children, they have affairs,' Vespasia pointed out sadly. 'I don't think I admire it, but I am quite aware that it occurs. I could name you half a dozen.'

'So could I,' Isobel agreed flippantly. 'We'll have to do it, and see if we know the same ones.'

Blanche Twyford was talking to Gwendolen, nodding every now and then, and Gwendolen was smiling. It was easy to guess the subject of their excitement.

Vespasia looked sideways at Isobel, and saw the shadow in her eyes again. If Bertie proposed marriage to Gwendolen this weekend, which seemed to be generally expected, would Isobel really lose more than a possible admirer? Did she care for him, perhaps even have hopes herself? She had loved her husband, Vespasia knew that, but he had been gone for three years now, and Isobel was a young woman, no more than Vespasia's own age. It was possible to fall in love again – in fact, at thirty it would be harsh and lonely not to.

Should she say something? Was this a time when real friendship dared embarrassment and rejection and spoke? Or kept silence and the pretence of not knowing, and allowed the deeper wounds to remain private?

The decision was taken from her by Lady Warburton joining them, and conversation moved to fashion, Prince Albert's latest ideas for improving the mind, and, of course, the Queen's enthusiasm for them. She seemed to agree with everything he said.

They were rejoined by the gentlemen, and the atmosphere changed again. Everyone became more self-conscious, backs a little straighter, laughter more delicate, movement more graceful. The servants had retreated to leave them alone. The final cleaning-up would be done when they retired to bed.

They were all facing Gwendolen and Bertie when Isobel made the remark. Gwendolen was sitting with her skirts swept around her like a tide, her head up, her slender throat pale in the candlelight. She looked beautiful and triumphant. Bertie stood close to her, just a little possessively.

'Charming,' Lady Warburton said very quietly, as if the announcement had already been made.

Vespasia looked at Isobel and saw the strain in her face. She felt a moment's deep sorrow for her. Whatever the prize, defeat has a bitter taste.

Peter Hanning was saying something trivial, and everyone laughed. There was a goblet of water on the side

14

table. Gwendolen asked for it.

Bertie reached across swiftly and picked it up, then set it on the tray, which had been left there. He passed it to her, balanced in one hand, bowing as he did so. 'Madam,' he said humbly. 'Your servant for ever.'

Gwendolen put out her hand.

'For heaven's sake, you look like a footman!' Isobel's voice was clear and brittle. 'Surely you aspire to be more than that? She's hardly going to give her favours to a servant! At least not to keep!'

The moment froze. It was a dreadful thing to have said, and Vespasia winced.

'She will require a gentleman,' Isobel went on. 'After all, Kilmuir could look forward to a title.' She turned to Gwendolen. 'Couldn't he?'

Gwendolen was white. 'I love the man,' she said huskily. 'The status means nothing to me.'

Isobel raised her eyebrows very high. 'You would give yourself to him if he were really a footman?' she asked incredulously. 'My dear, I believe you!'

Gwendolen stared at her, but her gaze was inward, as if she saw a horror beyond description, almost beyond endurance. Then slowly she rose to her feet, her eyes hollow. She seemed a trifle unsteady.

'Gwendolen!' Bertie said quickly, but she walked past him as if suddenly he were invisible to her. She stumbled to the door, needing a moment or two to grasp the handle and turn it, then went out into the hall.

Lady Warburton turned on Isobel. 'Really, Mrs Alvie, I

know you imagine that you are amusing, at least at times, but that remark merely exposed your envy, and it is most unbecoming.' She swivelled to face Omegus Jones. 'If you will excuse me, I shall make sure that poor Gwendolen is all right.' And with a crackle of skirts she swept out.

There was an uncomfortable silence. Vespasia decided to take control before the situation became irretrievable. She turned to Isobel. 'I don't think this can be salvaged with any grace. We would do better to retreat and leave well enough alone. Come. It is late anyway.'

Isobel hesitated only a moment, glancing at the ring of startled and embarrassed faces, and realised she could only agree.

Outside in the hall Vespasia took her arm, forcing her to stop before she reached the bottom of the stairs. 'What on earth has got hold of you?' she demanded. 'You will have to apologise to Gwendolen tomorrow, and to everyone else. Being in love with Bertie does not excuse what you did, and you would be a great deal better off if you had not made yourself so obvious!'

Isobel glared at her, her face ashen but for the high spots of colour in her cheeks, but she was too close to tears to answer. She was now perfectly aware of how foolish she had been, and that she had made not Gwendolen, but herself look vulnerable. She shook her arm free and stormed up the stairs without looking back.

Vespasia did not sleep well. Certainly Isobel had behaved

most unfortunately, but marriage, with love or without it, was a very serious business. For a woman it was the only honourable occupation, and battles for an eligible man of the charm and the financial means of someone like Bertie Rosythe were fought to the last ditch. She hurt for the pain Isobel must feel, and had just made it a great deal worse for herself. Vespasia could only imagine it. Her own marriage had been easily arranged. Her father was an earl, and she herself was startlingly beautiful. She could have been a duchess had she wished. She preferred a man of intelligence and an ambition to do something useful, and who had loved her for herself, and given her a great deal of freedom. It was a good bargain. The kind of love for which she hungered she had found in dreams, and hot Roman summers of manning the barricades against overwhelming odds. One loves utterly, and then yields to honour and duty, and returns home to live with other realities, leaving the height and the ache of passion behind.

When she rose in the morning, her maid assisted her to dress warmly in a blue-grey woollen gown against the December frost and a very sharp wind whining in the eaves and seeking to find every crack in the windows. She went downstairs to face the other guests, and whatever difficulties the night had not resolved.

She was met in the hall by Omegus Jones. He was wearing an outdoor jacket, and there was mud on his boots. His dark hair was untidy and his face was so pale he looked waxen.

'Vespasia . . .'

'Whatever is it?' She went to him immediately. 'You look ill! Can I help?' She touched his hand lightly. It was freezing – and wet. Suddenly she was frightened. Omegus, more than anyone else she knew, seemed always in control of himself, and of events. 'What is it?' she said again, more urgently.

He did not prevaricate. He closed his icy hand over hers with great gentleness. 'I am afraid we have just found Gwendolen's body in the lake.' He gestured vaguely behind him to the sheet of ornamental water beyond the sloping lawn, with its cedars and herbaceous border. 'We have brought her out, but there is nothing to be done for her. She seems to have been dead since some time last night.'

Vespasia was stunned. It was impossible. 'How can she have fallen in?' she said, denying the thought desperately. 'It is shallow at the edges. There are plants growing there, reeds! You would simply get stuck in the mud! And anyway, why on earth would she go walking down by the water on a December night? Why would anyone?'

Omegus looked totally serious, unmoved by her arguments, except to pity. Vespasia was touched by a deep fear.

'I'm sorry, my dear,' he answered, his eyes hollow. 'She went in from the bridge, where it is quite deep. The only conclusion possible seems to be that she jumped, of her own accord. The balustrade is quite high enough to prevent an accidental falling, even in the dark. I had them made that way myself.'

'Omegus! I'm so sorry!' Vespasia's first thought was for him, and the distress it would cause him, the dark shadow over the beauty of Applecross. It was a loveliness greater than simply that of a great house where art and nature had combined to create a perfect landscape of flowers, trees, water and views to the hills and fields beyond. Approached from the south-west along an avenue of towering elms, the classic Georgian façade looked towards the afternoon sun over the downs. The gravel forecourt was fronted by a balustrade, with a long, shallow flight of stone steps cutting between the banks down to the vast lawn, beyond which lay the ornamental water. It was a place of peace, where generations of love for the land had sunk into its fabric and left a residue of warmth, even in the starkness of winter.

'I'm afraid it will become most unpleasant,' he said unhappily. 'People will be frightened because sudden death of the young is a terrible reminder of the fragility of all life. She had seemed on the brink of new joy after her bereavement, and it has been snatched away from her. Only the boldest of us, and the least imaginative, do not sometimes, in the small hours of the morning, fear the same for ourselves. And they will not understand why it has happened. They will look for someone to blame, because anger is easier to live with than fear.'

'I don't understand!' she said with a gulp. 'Why on earth would she do such a thing? Isobel was cruel, but if anyone should be mortified, it is she! She betrayed her own vulnerability in front of those who will have no

19

understanding, and little mercy.'

'We know that, my dear Vespasia, but they do not,' he said softly, still touching her so lightly she felt only the coldness of his fingers. 'They will see only a woman with every cause to expect an offer of marriage, but who was publicly insulted by suggestions that she is a seeker after position, rather than a woman in love.' His face twisted with irony. 'Which is an absurd piece of hypocrisy, I am aware. We have created a society in which it is necessary for a woman to marry well if she is to succeed, because we have contrived for it to be impossible for her to achieve any safety or success alone, even should she wish to. But frequently we criticise most vehemently that which is largely our own doing.'

'Are you . . . are you saying that Isobel's remark drove Gwendolen to commit suicide?' Vespasia's voice cracked as if her mouth and throat were parched.

'It seems so,' he admitted. 'Unless there was an exchange between Bertie and Gwendolen after she left the withdrawing room, and a quarrel she did not feel she could repair.'

Vespasia could think of nothing to say. It was hideous.

'You offered to help me,' Omegus reminded her. 'I may ask that you do.'

'How?'

'I have very little idea,' he confessed. 'Perhaps that is why I need you.'

Vespasia swallowed hard. 'I shall tell Isobel,' she said, wondering how on earth she could make such a thing bearable. The day yawned ahead like an abyss, full of grief and confusion.

'Thank you,' he accepted. 'I shall have the servants ask everyone to be at breakfast, and tell them then.'

She nodded, then turned and went back upstairs and along to Isobel's room. She knocked on the door and waited until she heard Isobel's voice tell her to go in.

Isobel was lying in the bed, her dark hair spread across the pillow, her eyes shadowed around as if she too had slept badly. She sat up slowly, staring at Vespasia in surprise.

There was no mercy in hesitation. Vespasia sat on the bed facing Isobel. 'I have just met Omegus in the hall,' she began. 'They have found Gwendolen's body in the lake. The only conclusion possible from the circumstances is that some time after our unfortunate conversation in the withdrawing room she must have gone out alone and, in some derangement of mind, have jumped off the bridge. I'm afraid it is very bad.'

Isobel sat up, pulling the sheet around herself, even though the room was not cold. 'Is she . . .?'

'Of course. It is December! If she had not drowned she would have frozen.'

'But surely she must have fallen!' Isobel protested, pushing her hair off her face. 'Why on earth would she jump? That's ridiculous!' She shook her head. 'It can't be true!'

'If you remember, the balustrade along the bridge is too high to fall over by accident,' Vespasia reminded her.

'Anyway, why on earth would she be out there leaning over the bridge late on a December night? And alone!'

The little colour in Isobel's face had drained away, leaving her pasty-white. She started to shiver. Her hands were clenched in the sheets.

'Are you implying that my idiotic remark made her do that? Why? All I did was insult her! She wouldn't be the first woman to be called greedy, or desperate. That's absurd!' Her voice was sharp, a little high-pitched.

'Isobel, there is no point in pretending that it did not happen,' Vespasia said steadily, trying to sound reasonable, although she did not feel it. 'You are going to have to go down at some time, and face everyone, whatever they believe. And the longer you delay it, the more you will appear to be accepting the blame.'

'I'm not to blame!' Isobel said indignantly. 'I was rash in what I said, and I would have apologised to her today. But if she went and jumped off the bridge, that has nothing to do with me, and I won't have anyone say that it has!'

She flung the sheets aside and climbed out of the bed, stumbling a little as she stood up. She kept her back to Vespasia, as though blaming her for having brought the news. But Vespasia noticed that when she picked up her *peignoir* her fingers were stiff and it slipped out of her grasp, and it took her three attempts to retrieve it.

Breakfast was ghastly. When Vespasia and Isobel arrived everyone else was already gathered around the table and food was laid out on the sideboard in silver chafing dishes: finnan haddock, kedgeree, eggs, sausages, devilled kidneys, bacon, and of course plenty of fresh crisp toast, butter, marmalade and tea. People had taken some before Omegus Jones had told them what had occurred, but now nobody felt like eating.

Isobel's entrance had been greeted in silence, nor did anyone meet her eyes.

Vespasia looked at Omegus and saw the warning and the apology unspoken in his expression.

Isobel hesitated. No one was wearing black because they had not brought it, not foreseeing the occasion, and of course Isobel was the only one who had known of the death before dressing. She wore a sober dark green.

Lady Warburton was the first to acknowledge her presence, but it was with a chilly stare, her rather ordinary face pinched with distaste. She regarded Isobel's clothes first, long before her face. 'I see you were aware of the tragedy before you dressed,' she said coolly. 'In fact perhaps last night?'

'My dear Evelyn, do not let your grief . . .' Sir John began, then tailed away as his wife turned to glare at him.

'It is perfectly obvious she was aware of poor Gwendolen's death!' she said in a low, grating voice. 'Why else would she wear mourning to breakfast?'

'Hypocrite,' Blanche Twyford murmured half under her breath. No one doubted that she was referring to Isobel, not Lady Warburton.

Isobel pretended not to have heard. She took a slice of

toast, and then found herself unable to swallow it. She played with it for something to keep her hands occupied, and perhaps to prevent anyone else from noticing that they trembled.

Bertie looked haggard and utterly confused.

Vespasia wondered if he had gone after Gwendolen last night. Surely he must have. Or was it conceivable he had not? If he had followed her and told her of his feelings, asked her to marry him, as everyone had been expecting, nothing Isobel Alvie, or anyone else, could have said would have destroyed her happiness. Was that what he was thinking, that he avoided her eyes now? And what about Lady Warburton? *Had* she followed Gwendolen, or merely said she would, to escape the situation?

'This is perfectly dreadful!' Lady Salchester burst out. 'We really cannot sit here not knowing what has happened, and having no idea what to say to each other!'

'We know what has happened,' Blanche Twyford said angrily. 'Mrs Alvie spoke inexcusably last night, and poor Mrs Kilmuir was so distraught that she took her own life. It's as plain as the nose on your face.'

Lady Salchester froze. 'I beg your pardon?' she said, ice dripping from her voice.

'For heaven's sake!' Blanche flushed. 'I did not mean it personally. It is an expression – of clarity. We all know perfectly well what happened!'

'I don't,' Lord Salchester came surprisingly to his wife's aid. 'To me it is as much of a muddle as the nose on your face!'

Vespasia wanted to laugh, hysterically, and suppressed the desire with difficulty, holding her napkin to her lips and pretending to sneeze.

Blanche Twyford glared at Lord Salchester.

Salchester opened his blue eyes very wide. 'Why on earth should a perfectly healthy young woman on the brink of matrimony throw herself into the lake, merely because her rival insults her? I don't understand.' He looked baffled. He shook his head. 'Women,' he said unhappily. 'If she had been a chap she'd simply have insulted her back, and they'd have gone to bed friends.'

'Oh, do be quiet, Ernest!' Lady Salchester snapped at him. 'You are talking complete nonsense!'

'Am I?' he said mildly. 'Wasn't she going to be married? That's what everyone said.'

Bertie stood up, white-faced, and left the room.

'Good God! He's not going to the lake, is he?' Salchester asked, his napkin sliding to the floor.

Isobel left the table as well, only she went out of the other door, towards the garden, even though it was raining and not much above freezing outside.

'Guilt!' Lady Warburton said viciously.

'I think that's a little harsh,' Sir John expostulated. 'She was—'

'Both of them!' his wife interrupted, effectively cutting off whatever he had been going to say. He relapsed into silence.

Omegus rose to his feet. 'Lady Vespasia, I wonder if I might talk with you in the library?'

25

'Of course.' She was grateful for the chance to escape the ghastly meal table. She scraped her chair back before the footman could pull it out for her.

'You're not going to just leave it!' Lady Warburton accused her host. 'This cannot be run away from. I won't allow it!'

Omegus looked at her coldly. 'I am going to think before I act, Lady Warburton. An error now, even if made with the purest of motives, could cause grief which could not later be undone. Excuse me.' And leaving her angry, and now confounded, he left the room with Vespasia at his heels.

In the silence of the book-lined library, with its exquisite bronzes, he closed the door and turned to face her. 'Evelyn Warburton is right,' he said grimly. There was intense sadness is his eyes and the lines around his mouth were drawn down.

'It was foolish,' Vespasia agreed. 'And unkind. Both are faults, but not in any way crimes, or most of Society would be in prison. It is dreadful that Gwendolen should have taken her life, but surely it is because she believed that Bertie would not marry her after all. It cannot be simply that Isobel behaved so badly.'

He regarded her with patience. 'It is not necessarily what is, but what is perceived that Society will judge,' he answered. 'Whether it is fair or not will enter into it very little. If we allow the perception to pass without addressing it then each time the event is retold it will grow worse. What Isobel actually said will be lost in the exaggerations until no one remembers the truth. Tales alter every time they are retold, and, my dear, you must know that.' There was a faint reproof in his voice.

Of course she knew it, and felt the colour burn in her face for her evasion. 'What can we do?' she said helplessly. 'What do you suppose the truth is? And how will we ever know? Gwendolen can't tell us, and if Bertie quarrelled with her, do you imagine he will tell us, in view of what has happened? Did Lady Warburton go after her, do you know?'

'Apparently not. Do you know anything of medieval trial when someone was accused of a crime?' he asked.

Vespasia was astounded. Surely he could not have said what she thought she had heard. 'I beg your pardon?'

Somewhere in the garden a dog was barking, and a servant's rapid footsteps crossed the hall. The ghost of a smile curved Omegus' lips. 'I am not referring to trial by combat, or by ordeal. I was thinking of a process of discovering the truth so far as we are able, and if Isobel is indeed guilty of anything, or if Bertie is, then all of us agreeing upon a form of expiation which would absolve them of guilt, after which we would make a solemn covenant that the matter would be considered closed.'

A wild hope flared up inside her. 'But would we?' she said, struggling to believe it. 'Would we agree to it? And could we find the truth? What if the guilty person would not accept the expiation?' She lifted her shoulders very slightly. 'And what could it be? What if they simply walk away? We have no power to enforce anything. Why should they trust us to keep silent afterwards, let alone to forgive?'

He walked over to the heavy velvet curtains and the window overlooking the parkland, with its rolling grass and great trees, now winter bare. Rain spattered the glass.

'I have thought about it,' he said, as much to himself as to her. 'The idea always appealed to me, the belief in expiation and forgiveness, a new start. Surely that is the only hope for any of us. We need both to forgive and to be forgiven.'

Looking at him standing with the harsh light on his face Vespasia saw more pain inside him now than she had in all the years she had known him, and also a far greater understanding of peace. In that instant she wished above all to fulfil this faith in her, to make him pleased that it was she to whom he had turned.

'But why should they agree?' she said anxiously. 'We have no power other than persuasion.'

He smiled and turned to face her. 'Oh, but we have! The power of Society is almost infinite, my dear. To be excluded is a kind of death. And if one is spoken of with sufficient venom, invitations cease, doors are closed and one becomes invisible. People pass you by without a glance. You find that, in all ways that matter, you no longer exist. A young woman becomes unmarriageable, a young man has no career, no position, all clubs are closed to him.'

It was true. Vespasia had seen it. It was the cruellest fate because the people to whom it could happen were unfitted for any other life. They did not know how to earn a living in the work done by ordinary men and women. Those occupations also were closed to them. No woman born a lady could suddenly become a maid or a laundress. Even had she the skills, the temperament and the stamina, she was not acceptable either to an employer of the class she used to be, or to the other employees to whose class she did not belong, nor ever could.

And she was not fitted or trained for any of the other occupations in which a woman could earn her way.

Suddenly she realised just what might be ahead for Isobel, and she felt cold and sick. 'How will that help us?' she said huskily.

He looked at her with great earnestness. 'If I explain to everyone what I have in mind, and they agree, then they will all be bound by it,' he answered. 'The punishment for breaking their word would be exactly that same ostracism which will be applied to whoever is found at fault in Gwendolen's death. Anyone who refuses to abide by that brands themselves as outside the group of the rest of us. No one will wish to do that.' He shook his head a tiny fraction, lips tight. 'Don't tell me it is coercion. I know. Few people accept the judgement of their peers without it. It will offer a way for us to prevent the pain, and perhaps injustice, that may result otherwise.' His voice became softer. 'And as important, it will at least give Isobel, or Bertie if it is he to blame, a chance to expiate the act of cruelty they may have performed.'

'How?' she asked.

'Gwendolen left a letter behind,' he explained. 'It is sealed, and will remain so. It is addressed to her mother, Mrs Naylor, who lives near Inverness, in the far north of Scotland. We could post it, but that would be a harsh way for a mother to find out that her child has destroyed the life she laboured to give.'

Vespasia was appalled. 'You mean they would have to go to this unhappy woman and give her the letter? That's . . .' she was lost for words. Isobel would never do it! Neither would Bertie Rosythe. They would neither of them have the heart, or the stomach for it. Not to mention making the journey to the north of Scotland in December.

Omegus raised his eyebrows. 'Do you expect to be forgiven without pain, without a pilgrimage that costs the mind, the body and the heart?'

'I don't think it will work.'

'Will you at least help me try?'

She looked at him, standing lean, oddly graceful, the lines deeper in his face in the morning light, and she could not refuse. 'Of course.'

'Thank you,' he said solemnly.

'What?' Lord Salchester said with stinging disbelief when they were gathered together at the luncheon table. The first course was finished when Omegus requested their attention and began to explain to them his plan.

'Preposterous!' Lady Warburton agreed. 'We all know perfectly well what happened. For heaven's sake, we saw it!'

'Heard it,' Sir John corrected.

She glared at him.

'Actually,' he went on, 'it's not a bad idea at all.'

Lady Warburton swung round in her chair and fixed him with a glacial eye. 'It is ridiculous. And if we find Mrs Alvie guilty, as we will do, what difference will that make?'

'That is not the end of the issue,' Omegus cut across her. Vespasia saw him struggling to keep the dislike from his face. 'In medieval times not all crimes were punished by execution or imprisonment,' he went on. 'Sometimes the offender was permitted to make a pilgrimage of expiation. If they returned, which, in those dangerous times, very often they did not, then the sin was considered to have been washed out. All men were bound to pardon it, and take the person back among them as if it had not occurred. It was never spoken of again, and he was trusted and loved as before.'

'A pilgrimage?' Peter Hanning said with disbelief, derision close to laughter in his voice. 'To where, for heaven's sake? Walsingham? Canterbury? Jerusalem, perhaps? Anyway, travel is a relative pleasure these days, if one can afford it. I'm not a religious man. I don't care a fig if Mrs Alvie, or anyone else, makes a journey to some holy place.'

'You have missed the point, Peter,' Omegus told him. 'I shall choose the journey, and it will not be a pleasure, nor will it be particularly expensive. But it will be extremely difficult, particularly so for anyone who bears guilt at all

31

for the death of Gwendolen Kilmuir. And if we profess any claim to justice whatever, we will not decide in advance who that is.'

'I agree,' Sir John said immediately.

'So do I,' Vespasia added. 'I agree to both justice and forgiveness.'

'And if I don't?' Lady Warburton asked sharply, looking across at Vespasia, her brow creased with dislike, her mouth pinched.

Vespasia smiled. 'Then one would be compelled to wonder why not,' she replied.

'I agree,' Blanche Twyford said. 'Then the matter need never be spoken of beyond these walls. It will stop gossip among others who were not here, and any slander they may make against any of us, letting their imaginations build all manner of speculation. If we are all bound by what we agree, and the punishment is carried out here, the matter is ours. Surely you agree, don't you?'

'I suppose if you put it that way . . .' Lady Warburton said reluctantly.

Lord Salchester agreed also.

Omegus looked at Bertie, the question in his face.

'Who is to be the judge of this?' Bertie asked dubiously. Today his elegance seemed haggard, his exquisite suit and cravat in irrelevance.

'Omegus,' Vespasia said before anyone else could speak. 'He is not involved and we may trust him to be fair.'

'May we?' Bertie said. 'Applecross is his house. He is most certainly involved.'

'He is not involved in Gwendolen's death.' Vespasia kept her temper with increasing difficulty. 'Do you have someone in mind you prefer?'

'I think the whole idea is absurd,' he replied. 'And totally impractical.'

'I disagree,' Lord Salchester spoke with sudden decisiveness, his voice sharp. 'I think it is an excellent idea. I am quite happy to be bound by it. So is my wife.' He did not consult her. 'It will be for the good of all our reputations, and will allow the matter to be dealt with immediately, and justice be served.' He looked a little balefully around the table at the others. 'Who is against it? Apart from those either guilty, or too short-sighted to see the ultimate good.'

Omegus smiled bleakly, but he did not point out the loaded nature of the challenge. One by one they all agreed, except Isobel.

Vespasia looked at her very steadily. 'Any alternative would be much worse, I believe,' she said softly. 'Do we all give our word, on pain of being ostracised ourselves should we break it, that we will keep silent, absolutely, on the subject after the judgment is given, and should the price be paid? Then the offender, if there is one, begins anew from the day of his or her return, and we forget the offence as if it had not happened?'

One by one, reluctantly at first, they gave their pledges.

'Thank you,' Omegus said gravely. 'Now, if you will excuse me, I have more personal arrangements to make sure of for Gwendolen.' His face pinched with sadness. 'I would like it to be as . . . gentle as possible.'

They collected in the withdrawing room, the curtains open on the formal garden sweeping down towards the wind-ruffled water of the lake, and the trees beyond. It was the place where they could all be seated in something close to a circle, and the servants were dismissed until they should be called for. No one was to interrupt.

Omegus called them to order, then asked each of them in turn to tell what they knew of Gwendolen Kilmuir's actions, her feelings, and what she may have said to them of her hopes from the time she had arrived three days before.

They began tentatively, unsure how far to trust, but gradually emotions were stirred by memory.

'She was full of hope,' Blanche said a little tearfully. 'She believed that her time of loss was coming to an end.' She shot a look of intense dislike at Isobel. 'Kilmuir's death was a terrible blow to her.'

'So much so that she intended to marry less than a year and a half later,' Peter Hanning observed, leaning back in his chair, his cravat a little crooked, a slight curl to his lip.

'They had had some difficult times,' Blanche explained crossly. 'He was not an easy man.'

'It was she who was not an easy woman,' Fenton Twyford interrupted. 'She took some time to accept her responsibilities. Kilmuir was very patient with her, but the time came when he bore it less graciously.'

'A great deal less graciously,' Blanche agreed. 'But he

was mending his ways. She was looking forward to a far greater warmth between them when he was killed.'

'Killed?' Sir John said abruptly.

'In a driving accident,' Blanche told him. When she heard of it poor Gwendolen was devastated. That was why it was so wonderful that she had a second chance at happiness.' She looked at Bertie with intense meaning.

He blushed miserably.

The tale progressed, each person adding his or her own piece until a picture was built up of the courtship of Bertie and Gwendolen reaching the point when everyone expected an announcement. More than one person had noticed that Isobel was not pleased, even though she attempted to hide the fact. Now all the thoughts came to the surface, and she was clearly humiliated, but she did not dare escape. It would have been an admission, and she was determined not to make one.

But the tide swept relentlessly on; even Vespasia was carried along by it until she was placed in a position where she must speak either for Isobel, or against her. Vespasia had been forced to see more clearly now than at the time how deep the feelings had been, on both sides. Under the veneer of wit and a kind of friendship there had been a struggle for victory, which would have lifted either one woman or the other back into the centre of Society, assured of comfort and acceptance. The other would be left among the number of women alone, always a little apart, a little lost, hoping for the next invitation, but never certain that it would come, dreading the next bill in case it would not be met, mending and making do.

Without realising why, Vespasia spoke for Isobel. Gwendolen was beyond her help, and many others were eager to take her part.

'We use what arts we have,' she said, looking more at Omegus than the others. 'Gwendolen was pretty and charming. She flattered people by allowing them to help her, and she was grateful. Isobel was far too proud for that, and too honest. She used wit, and sometimes it was cruel. I think when Gwendolen was the victim she affected to be more wounded than she was. She craved sympathy and she won it. Isobel was foolish enough not to see that.'

'If Gwendolen was not really hurt, why did she kill herself?' Blanche demanded angrily, challenge in her eyes and the set of her thin shoulders. 'That seems to be taking the cry for sympathy rather too far to be of any use!' Her voice was heavily sarcastic, her smile a sneer.

Vespasia looked at Bertie. 'When Gwendolen left last night, after Isobel's remark, did you go after her to see if she was all right?' she asked him. 'Did you assure her that you did not for an instant believe she was in love with your money and position rather than with you?'

Bertie coloured painfully and his face tightened.

Everyone waited.

'Did you?' Omegus said in a very clear voice.

Bertie looked up. 'No. I admit it, Isobel spoke with such . . . certainty, I did wonder. I, God forgive me, I doubted her.' He fidgeted. 'I started to think of things she had said, things other people had said, warnings.' He tried to laugh and failed. 'Of course I realise now that they were merely malicious, born of jealousy. But last night I hesitated. If I hadn't, poor Gwendolen would be alive, and I should not be alone, mourning her loss.' The look he gave Isobel was venomous in its intensity, and its blame.

Vespasia was stunned. It was the last response she had intended to provoke. Far from helping Isobel she had sealed her fate.

Omegus also looked wretched, but he was bound by his own rules.

The verdict was a matter of form. By overwhelming majority they found Isobel guilty of unbridled cruelty and deliberate intent to ruin Gwendolen, falsely, in the eyes of the man she loved. There was sympathy for Bertie, but it was not unmixed with a certain contempt.

'And what is this pilgrimage that Mrs Alvie is to make?' Fenton Twyford asked angrily. 'I must say I agree with Peter. I really don't care where she goes, as long as it is not across my path. I can't stand a woman with a vicious tongue. It's inexcusable.'

'Very little is inexcusable,' Omegus said with sudden cutting authority, his face at once bleak and touched with a terrible compassion. 'You have given your word before everyone here that if she completes the journey you will wipe the matter from your memory as if it did not happen – otherwise you will have broken your word, and that also cannot be excused. If a man's oath does not bind him, then he cannot be a part of any civilised society.'

Twyford went white. He glanced around the table. No one smiled at him.

Lord Salchester nodded in agreement. 'Quite so,' he said. 'Quite so.'

'Are we agreed?' Omegus enquired softly.

'We are,' came the answer from everyone except Isobel.

Omegus turned to her and waited.

'What journey?' she said huskily.

Omegus explained. 'Gwendolen left a letter addressed to her mother, Mrs Naylor. I have not opened it, nor will you. It's obviously private. You will take it to Mrs Naylor and explain to her that Gwendolen has taken her own life, and your part in it. If Mrs Naylor wishes to come to London, or to Applecross, you will accompany her, unless she will not permit you to. But you will do all in your power to succeed. She lives near Inverness, in the Highlands of Scotland. Her address is on the envelope.'

There was total silence in the room. The sound of a sudden shower lashing the windows was loud.

'I won't!' Isobel said in a rush of outrage. 'The north of Scotland! At this time of year? And to . . . to face . . . absolutely not.' She pushed her chair back, and stood up, her body shaking, her face burning with hectic colour. 'I will not do it.' For a moment she stared at them, and then left the room, flinging wide the door so that it slammed against the further wall, then swung shut after her.

Vespasia half rose also, then realised the futility of it and sat down again.

'I thought she wouldn't,' Lady Warburton said with a smile of satisfaction.

Vespasia envisaged for an instant a crocodile who fears it is robbed of its prey, and then feels its teeth sink into flesh after all. 'You must be pleased,' she said aloud. 'I imagine you would have found it nigh on impossible to know something unkind about someone, and be unable to repeat it to others.'

Lady Warburton looked at her coldly, her face suddenly bloodless, eyes glittering. 'I would be more careful in my choice of friends, if I were you, Lady Vespasia. Your father's title will not protect you for ever. There is a degree of foolishness beyond which even you will have to pay.'

'You are suggesting I desert my friends the moment it becomes inconvenient for me?' Vespasia enquired, although there was barely a lift of question in her tone, only heavy disgust. 'Why does it not astound me that you should say so?' She also rose to her feet. 'Excuse me,' she said to no one in particular, and left the room.

Outside in the hall she was completely alone. There was no servant in sight, no footman waiting to be called. They had taken Omegus' request for privacy as an absolute order. There was something strangely judicial about it, as if everything, even domestic detail, might be different from now on.

She crossed the parquet and climbed slowly up the great staircase. A few words had changed everything. But they were not merely words, they sprang from thoughts and passions, deep tides that had been there all the time;

it was only the knowledge of them that was new.

Vespasia found it difficult to concentrate on dressing for dinner. Her maid suggested one gown after another, but nothing seemed appropriate, nor, for once, did she really care. The silks, laces, embroidery, the whole palette of subtle and gorgeous colours seemed an empty pleasure. Gwendolen was dead, from whatever despair, real or imagined, that had gripped her, and Isobel was on the brink of suffering more than she yet understood.

Vespasia thought everyone else would be dressing soberly, in grief for Gwendolen, and in parade of their sense of social triumph, sombre but victorious. She decided to wear purple. It suited her porcelain skin and the shimmering glory of her hair. It would be beautiful, appropriate for half-mourning, and outrageous for a woman of her youth. Altogether it would serve every purpose.

She swept down the stairs again, as she had only an evening ago, to gasps of surprise, and either admiration or envy, depending upon whether it was Lord Salchester or Lady Warburton. The merest glance told her that Isobel was not yet there. Would she have the courage to come?

Omegus was at her elbow, his face carefully smoothed of expression, but she could not mistake the anxiety in his eyes.

'She is not going to run away, is she?' he said so quietly that Blanche Twyford, only a yard or two from them, could not have heard.

Vespasia had exactly the same fear. 'I don't know,' she admitted. 'I think she is very angry. There is a certain injustice in putting the blame entirely upon her. If Bertie was so easily put off, then he did not love Gwendolen with much depth, or honour.'

'Of course not, my dear,' Omegus murmured. 'Surely that is the disillusion which really hurt Gwendolen more than she could bear?'

Suddenly it made agonising sense. It was not any suggestion Isobel made that had destroyed her, it was the exposing of the shallowness beneath the dreams, the breaking of the thin veneer of hope with which Gwendolen had deceived herself. She had not lost the prize, she had seen that it did not exist, not as she needed it to be.

'Was that really a cruelty?' she said aloud, meeting his eyes for the first time in their whispered conversation.

Omegus did not hesitate. 'Yes,' he answered. 'There are some things to which we need to wake up slowly, and the weaknesses of someone we love are among them.'

'But surely she needed to see what a frail creature he is before she married him!' Vespasia protested.

He smiled. 'Oh, please think a little longer, a little more deeply, my dear.'

She was surprisingly cut – not bluntly as by a knife, but deeply and almost without realising it for the first few seconds, as a razor cuts. She had not been aware until this moment how much she cared what Omegus thought of her.

41

Perhaps he saw the change in her face. His expression softened.

She found herself pulling away, her pride offended that he should see his power to wound her.

He saw that too, and he ignored it. 'She would have accepted him,' he said, still quietly. 'She had no better offer, and by the time she had realised his flaws, he might have begun to overcome them, and habit, tenderness, other promises made and kept, might have blunted the edge of disappointment and given other compensations that would have been enough.' He put his hand on her arm, so lightly she saw it rather than felt it. 'Love is not perfection,' he said. 'It is tolerance, dreams past and the future shared. A great deal of it, my dear, is friendship, if it is to last. There is nothing more precious than true friendship. It is the rock upon which all other loves must stand if they are to endure. She should have made her own decision, not have it made for her by someone else's desperate realisation of defeat.'

She did not answer. His words filled her mind and left no room for any of her own.

Ten minutes later when Isobel still had not appeared, Vespasia decided to go to fetch her. She went back up the stairs and along the west corridor to Isobel's room. She knocked, and when there was no answer, turned the handle and went in.

Isobel was standing before the long glass, looking critically at herself. She was not beautiful, but she had a great grace, and in her bronze and black gown she looked magnificent, more striking, more dramatic than Gwendolen ever had. Vespasia saw for the first time that that was precisely the trouble. Bertie Rosythe did not want a dramatic wife. He might like to play with fire, but he did not wish to live with it. Isobel could never have won.

'If you do not come now, you are going to be late,' Vespasia said calmly.

Isobel swung round, startled. She had obviously expected her maid returning.

'I haven't decided if I am coming yet,' she replied. 'I didn't hear you knock!'

'I dare say you were too deep in your own thoughts,' Vespasia brushed it aside. 'You must come,' she insisted. 'If you don't you will be seen as having run away, and that would be an admission of guilt.'

'They think I am guilty anyway,' Isobel said bitterly. 'Don't pretend you cannot see that! Even you with so . . .'

Vespasia had been at fault. 'I did not intend my remarks to give them that opening,' she answered. 'I am truly sorry for that. It was far clumsier than I meant it to be.'

Isobel kept her head turned away. 'I dare say they would have come to the same place anyway, just taken a little longer. But it would have been easier for me had the final blow not come from a friend.'

'Then you may consider yourself avenged,' Vespasia said. 'I am suitably chastened, and found guilty of my own sin. Are you now coming down to dinner? The longer you leave it, the more difficult it will be. That is the truth, whoever is to blame for anything.'

Isobel turned her head very slowly. 'Why are you wearing purple, for heaven's sake? Is anyone else in mourning?'

Vespasia smiled bleakly. 'Of course not. No one foresaw the necessity of bringing it. I am wearing purple because it suits me.'

'Everything suits you!' Isobel retorted.

'No it doesn't. Everything I wear suits me, because I chose not to wear what doesn't. Now put on your armour, and come to dinner.'

'Armour!'

'Courage, dignity, hope – and enough sense not to speak unless you are spoken to, and not to try to be funny.'

'Funny! I couldn't laugh if Lord Salchester performed handstands on the lawn!'

'You could if Lady Warburton choked on the soup.'

Isobel smiled wanly. 'You're right,' she agreed. 'I could.'

But dinner was a nightmare. No one greeted Isobel when she came down the stairs, except Omegus. It was as if they had not seen her, even though she descended the great staircase, dark blue satins rustling, and the outswept edge of her skirts actually brushed those of Blanche Twyford, because she did not move to allow her past. The moment later, as Vespasia approached, she stepped aside graciously.

The conversation did not hesitate, but Isobel was not

included. She spoke once, but no one appeared to hear her.

When the butler announced that dinner was served, Omegus offered her his arm because it was apparent that no other man was going to. Once they were seated, Lady Warburton looked at Lady Vespasia, then at Omegus.

'Am I mistaken, Mr Jones, or did you lay down the rules of this medieval trial of yours with the intention that we were all to be bound by them, or our own honour was also forfeit?'

'I did, Lady Warburton,' he replied.

'Then perhaps you would explain them to me again. You seem to be flouting what I understood you to say.' She looked meaningfully at Isobel, then back again at Omegus with wide challenging gaze.

He coloured very faintly. 'You are right, Lady Warburton,' he conceded. 'I am as bound as anyone else, but I am still hoping that Mrs Alvie will reconsider her refusal, and then a final decision must be made. I choose to wait until then before I act.'

'I suppose you have that privilege,' she said grudgingly. 'At least while we are at Applecross.'

The meal began, and Isobel was served exactly as everyone else was, but when she requested that the salt be passed to her, Fenton Twyford, who was next to her, looked across the table at Peter Hanning, and asked his opinion on the likely winner of the Derby next year.

'Would you be kind enough to pass me the salt?' Isobel replied.

'I must say I disagree,' Twyford said loudly in the silence. 'I think that colt of Bamburgh's will take it. What do you think, Rosythe?'

Isobel did not ask again.

The rest of the meal proceeded in the same way. She was ignored as if her seat were empty. People spoke of Christmas, and of next year, who would attend what function during the Season – balls, races, regattas, garden parties, exhibitions, riding in Rotten Row, walking in the botanical gardens, the opera, the theatre, pleasure cruises down the Thames. No one asked Isobel where she was going. They behaved as if she would not be there. There was no grief as if for the dead, as when Gwendolen's name was mentioned; it was not simply a ceasing to be, but as if she had never been.

She remained at the table, growing paler and paler. Vespasia walked beside her when the ladies withdrew to leave the gentlemen to their port. It was painful to remember that this time yesterday Gwendolen had been with them. None of the tragedy had happened. Now she was lying in one of the unused morning rooms, and tomorrow the undertaker would come to dress her for the grave.

Perhaps they guessed that it was the closeness of the hour to the event, but as the women entered the withdrawing room each one fell silent. Vespasia found herself shivering. Death was not a stranger to any of them. There were many diseases, the risks of childbirth, the accidents of even quite ordinary travel, but this was different, and the darkness of it touched them all.

Within twenty minutes of the door closing Isobel rose to her feet, and since they had not acknowledged her presence, she did not bother to excuse her leaving. She went out in silence.

Vespasia followed almost immediately. Not only did she need to see Isobel and try in every way she could to persuade her to make the journey to Scotland, she felt she could not bear to stay any longer in the withdrawing room with the other women, and listen to their gloating. There was something repellent in their relishing of Isobel's downfall and the doling out of punishment, because it had nothing to do with justice, or the possibility of expiation. It was to do with personal safety, and the satisfaction of being one of the included, not of those shut out.

Vespasia went back across the hallway, greeted courteously by the butler. She wished him good night, wondering how awkward it was going to be for the domestic staff to work their way through the silences and rebuffs, and decide whose leads to follow. Perhaps the real question was, how long would Omegus hold out against his own edict?

At the top of the stairs she retraced her path along the west wing and knocked on Isobel's door.

Again her knock was not answered, and again she went in.

Isobel was standing in the middle of the floor, her body stiff, her face white with misery. 'Don't you ever wait to be invited?' she said, her voice husky and on the edges of losing control.

Vespasia closed the door behind her. 'I don't think I can afford to wait,' she replied.

Isobel took a deep breath, steadying herself with a visible effort. 'And what can you possibly say that matters?' she asked.

Vespasia swept her considerable skirt to one side and sat down on the bedroom chair, as if she intended to stay for some time. 'Do you intend to accept virtual banishment? And don't delude yourself that it will only be by those who are here this weekend, because it will not. They will broadcast their version of the truth as soon as they return to London. By next Season all Society will have one version of it or another. If you are honest, you know that is true.'

Isobel's eyes swam with tears, but she refused to give way to them. 'Are you going to suggest that I accept the blame for Gwendolen's death and take this wretched letter to her mother?' she said, her voice choking. 'All I did was imply that she was ambitious, which was perfectly true. Most women are. We have to be.'

'You were cruel, and funny at her expense.' Vespasia added the further truth: 'You implied she was ambitious, but also that her love for Bertie would cease to exist were he in a different social class, or financial.'

Isobel's dark eyes widened. 'And you are claiming that it would not? You believe she would marry a greengrocer, or a footman?'

'Of course not,' Vespasia said impatiently. 'To begin with, no greengrocer or footman would ask her. The point is irrelevant. Your remark was meant to crush her and make her look greedy, and more importantly, to make Bertie see her love for him as merely opportunism. Don't be disingenuous, Isobel.'

Isobel glared at her, but she was too close to losing control to trust herself to speak.

'Anyway,' Vespasia went on briskly, 'none of it matters very much . . .'

'Is that what you intruded into my bedroom to tell me?' Isobel gasped, the tears brimming over and running down her cheeks. 'Get out! You are worse than they are! I imagined you were my friend and, my God, how mistaken I was. You are a total hypocrite!'

Vespasia remained exactly where she was. She did not even move enough to rustle the silk of her gown. 'What matters,' she said steadily, 'is that we face the situation as it is, and deal with it. There is none of them interested in the truth, and it is unlikely we will ever know exactly why Gwendolen killed herself, far less prove it to people who do not wish to know. But Omegus has offered you a chance not only to expiate whatever guilt you might have, but to retain your position in Society, and oblige everyone here to keep absolute silence about it, or face ostracism themselves – which is a feat of genius, I believe.' She smiled very slightly. 'And if you succeed, you will have the pleasure of watching them next Season watching you, and being unable to say a word. Lady Warburton and Blanche Twyford will find it extremely hard. They will suffer every moment of forced civility in silence. That alone should be of immeasurable satisfaction to you. It will be to me!'

Isobel smiled a little tremulously. She took a shuddering breath. 'All the way to Inverness?'

'There will be trains,' Vespasia responded. 'The line goes that far now.'

Isobel looked away. 'That will be the least part of it. I dare say it will take days, and be cold and uncomfortable, with infinite stops. But facing that woman, and giving her Gwendolen's letter, which might say anything about me! And having to wait and watch her grief? It will be . . . unbearable!'

'It will be hard, it will not be unbearable,' Vespasia corrected.

Isobel stared at her furiously. 'Would you do it? And don't you dare lie to me!'

Vespasia heard her own voice with amazement. 'I will do. I'll come with you.'

Isobel blinked. 'Really? You promise?'

Vespasia breathed in and out slowly. What on earth had she committed herself to? She was not guilty of any offence towards Gwendolen Kilmuir. But had that really anything to do with it? Neither guilt nor deserving were really the issue. Friendship was – and need. 'Yes,' she said. 'I'll come with you. We shall set off tomorrow morning. We will have to go to London first, of course, and then take the next train to Scotland. We will deliver the letter to Mrs Naylor, and accompany her back here if she will allow us to. Omegus said nothing to the effect that you had to go alone, simply that you had to go.'

'Thank you,' Isobel said, the tears running unchecked down her face. 'Thank you very much.'

Vespasia stood up. 'We shall tell them tomorrow morning at breakfast. Have your maid pack, and dress for travelling. Wear your warmest suit, and best boots. There will probably be snow further north, and it is bound to be colder. Sleep well tonight.'

Isobel sniffed, and gave a little groan.

Vespasia's mind whirled with the enormity of her decision. She did actually sleep quite well, but her dreams were of roaring trains and wind and snow-swept landscapes, and a grief-stricken and unforgiving woman bereft of her child.

She woke with a headache, dressed for travel and left her maid packing while she went down to breakfast.

Everyone was assembled, ready to begin the day's deliberate ostracism again. The dining room was warm, the fire lit and the sideboard laden with silver dishes from which delicious aromas emanated. Only Omegus looked distinctly unhappy. Almost immediately he caught Vespasia's eye and she smiled at him, giving an imperceptible nod. She saw the answering flash of light in his eyes, and his body eased, his right hand unclenched where it lay on the fresh linen of the table.

Isobel came in almost on her heels, as if she had been waiting.

Everyone wished Vespasia good morning and asked if she were well, and if her night had been restful. They ignored Isobel as if she had not been there. And this time she did not speak, but took her place at the table with a calm, pale face, and began to eat after helping herself from the toast rack and the teapot.

Peter Hanning mentioned the weather, and invited Bertie to a game of billiards in the afternoon. Lord Salchester announced that he was going for a walk. Lady Salchester said that she would accompany him, which took the smile from his face.

Isobel finished her toast and stood up, turning to Omegus.

'Mr Jones, I have given your offer much serious thought. I was mistaken to refuse it. A chance to redeem oneself, and have past errors forgotten as if they had not existed, is something given far too rarely, and should not be declined. I shall leave Applecross this morning, taking the letter to Mrs Naylor with me, and I shall catch the first available train to Scotland and deliver it to her. If she will accept my company on the return, then I shall do that also. When we reach London again I shall inform you of the outcome, and trust that everyone here will keep their word according to our bond.'

Lady Warburton looked crestfallen, as if she had lifted a particularly delicate morsel to her lips, only to have it fall off on to the floor as she opened her mouth to eat it.

The ghost of a smile touched Isobel's face.

'How shall we know that you gave the letter to Mrs Naylor, and did not merely say that you did?' Lady Warburton asked irritably.

'You will have Mrs Alvie's word for it,' Omegus answered coldly.

'You will also have Mrs Naylor's word, should you wish to ask her,' Isobel pointed out.

'Really!' Lady Warburton subsided into indignant silence.

'Bravo,' Lord Salchester said softly. 'You have courage, my dear. It will not be a comfortable journey.'

'It will be abysmal!' Fenton Twyford added. 'Inverness could be knee-deep in snow, and the shortest day of the year is less than three weeks away. In the far north of Scotland that could mean hardly any daylight at all. You do realise Inverness is another hundred and fifty miles north of Edinburgh, I suppose? At least!'

'What if your train gets stuck in a snowdrift?' Blanche asked hopefully.

'It is the beginning of December, not mid-January,' Sir John Warburton pointed out. 'It could be perfectly pleasant. Inverness-shire is a fine county.'

Lady Warburton looked surprised. 'When were you ever there?'

He smiled. 'Oh, once or twice. So was Fenton, you know.'

'Doing what?'

'Wonderful country for walking.'

'In December?' Hanning's eyebrows shot up and his voice was sharp with disbelief.

'It hardly matters,' Vespasia interrupted. 'Now is when we are going. We shall leave as soon as our packing is completed, if the trap can be arranged to take us to the railway station.'

'You are leaving as well?' Lord Salchester said with clear disappointment.

Omegus looked at Vespasia.

'Yes,' she replied.

Isobel smiled, pride in her face, and a shadow of uncertainty. 'Lady Vespasia has offered to come with me.'

Omegus smiled, a sweet, shining look that lit his face, making him beautiful.

'To give the letter to Mrs Naylor if Mrs Alvie should lose her nerve?' Blanche Twyford said bitingly. 'That hardly makes of it the ordeal it is supposed to be!' She turned to Omegus. 'Are we still bound by our oaths, in spite of this new turn of events?'

Omegus replied, 'In the medieval trials of which I spoke, and upon which I have modelled my plan, the accused person was permitted friends to speak for them, and the friend risked facing the same punishment along with them. If found guilty, the accused person promised to undertake the pilgrimage assigned, and if their friend were sure enough of their worth, had the courage and the selflessness to go with them, then that was the greatest mark of friendship that they could show. Neither the physical hardship nor the spiritual journey will be lessened, nor the threats that face them along the way. They will simply face them together, rather than alone. And the answer to your question, Mrs Twyford is, yes, you are just as bound.'

'Remarkable,' Lord Salchester said to Vespasia, with very obvious admiration. 'I admire your loyalty, my dear.'

'Stubbornness,' Lady Warburton said under her breath. Bertie looked everywhere but at Isobel.

Vespasia turned to Omegus and found him gazing back at her with a happiness that she found suddenly and startlingly disconcerting. She even wondered for a moment if she had made the rash promise for Isobel's sake, or just so she could see that look in Omegus' eyes. Then she dismissed that as absurd, and finished her breakfast.

The lady's maids would follow later with their mistresses' luggage, and remain at their respective houses in London. The expiatory journey was to be made alone. It would be both unfair and compromising to the integrity of the oath were they to have gone as well. They did not deserve the hardship, nor were they party to any agreement of silence.

The travellers departed just after ten o'clock, with ample time to catch the next train to London. Omegus saw them off at the front door, his hair whipped by the fresh, hard wind that blew off the sweeping parkland with the clean smell of rain.

'I shall be waiting for your word from London,' he said quietly. 'I wish you God's speed.'

'Are you quite sure it is acceptable for Vespasia to come with me? I have no intention of making this journey only to discover at the end that it doesn't count.'

'It counts,' he assured her. 'Do not underestimate the

difficulties ahead just because you are not alone. Vespasia may ease some of them for you, both by her presence and her wit and courage, but it is you who must face Mrs Naylor. Should she do that for you, then indeed you will not have made your expiation. If you should lie, Society may forgive you, unable to prove your deceit, but you will know, and that is what matters in the end.'

'I won't lie!' Isobel said stiffly, anger tight in her voice.

'Of course you will not,' he agreed. 'And Vespasia will be your witness, in case Mrs Naylor is not inclined to be.'

Isobel bit her lip. 'I admit, I had not thought of that. I suppose it would not be surprising. I . . . I wish I knew what that letter said!'

His face shadowed. 'You cannot,' he said with a note of warning. 'I am afraid that uncertainty is part of your journey. Now you must go, or you may miss the train. It is a long wait until the next one.' He turned to Vespasia. 'Much will happen to you before I see you again, my dear. Please God, the harvest of it will be good. God's speed.'

'Goodbye, Omegus,' she answered, accepting his hand to climb up into the trap and seat herself with the rug wrapped around her knees.

The groom urged the pony forward as Isobel clasped her hands in front of her, staring ahead into the wind, and Vespasia turned once to see Omegus still standing in the doorway, a slender figure, arms by his sides, but still watching them until they went round the corner of the driveway and the great elm trunks closed him from sight.

★ ★ ★

The train journey to London seemed tedious, but it was in fact very short, little more than two hours, compared with the forthcoming journey northwards. In London they took separate hansoms to their individual houses in order to pack more suitable clothes for the next step. Evening gowns would not be needed – and there would be no lady's maids to care for them – but additional winter skirts and heavier jackets, boots and capes most definitely would. They agreed to meet at Euston Station preparatory to catching the train northbound at six o'clock that evening.

Vespasia arrived first, and was angry with herself for being anxious in case Isobel at the last moment lost her nerve. She paced back and forth on the freezing platform. Odd how railway stations always seemed to funnel the wind until it increased its strength and its biting edge to twice whatever it was anywhere else! And, of course, the air was full of steam, flying smuts of soot, and the noise – shouting, doors clanging to, and people coming and going.

Then fifteen minutes before the train was due to depart, she saw Isobel's tall figure sweeping ahead of a porter with her baggage, her head jerking from right to left as she searched for Vespasia, obviously afflicted by the same fear of facing the journey, and its more dreadful arrival, alone.

'Thank heavens!' she said, her voice shaking with intense relief as she saw Vespasia. She waved her arm at the porter. 'Thank you! This will be excellent. Please put them aboard for me.' And she opened her reticule to find an appropriate reward for him.

'Did you doubt me?' Vespasia asked her.

'Of course not,' Isobel said with feeling. 'Did you doubt me?'

'Of course not,' Vespasia replied, smiling.

'Liar!' Isobel smiled back. 'It's going to be awful, isn't it!' It was not a question.

'I should think so,' Vespasia agreed. 'Do you wish to turn back?'

Isobel pulled a rueful face, and there was honesty, and fear, in her eyes. 'I would love to, but it would be worse in the end. Besides, I told those wretched people that I would. I sealed my fate then. Nothing this could do to me would be worse than facing them if I fail!'

'Of course. That was the whole purpose of saying it at the breakfast table, surely?' Vespasia stopped the porter and added her financial appreciation as he loaded her luggage as well, just one case – more and warmer clothes, in case they should be needed. If they were fortunate, the whole mission could be accomplished in one day, and they would be able to return. The long weekend at Applecross would be barely finished before they were in London again.

The train pulled out with whistles and clangs and much belching of steam. Slowly it picked up speed through the city, past serried rows of rooftops, then green spaces, factories, more houses, and eventually out into the open countryside, now patched with the dark turned earth of ploughed fields, and the scattered leafless copses of woodland. The rhythm of the wheels over the track would have been soothing to the two travellers, were they going anywhere else.

The winter afternoon faded quickly, and it was not more than an hour before they were rushing through the night, the steam past the window reduced to the red lines from lit sparks at speed, everything else a blur of darkness.

They stopped regularly, to set down passengers or to pick up more, and of course to allow people to stretch their legs, avail themselves of necessary facilities, and purchase refreshments of one sort and another.

Vespasia tried to sleep through as much of the night as she could. The movement of the train was pleasant and kept up a steady kind of music, but sitting more or less upright was far from comfortable. She was aware of Isobel watching the lights of stations and towns pass by with their steady progress northwards, and knew she must dread their arrival. But they had exhausted discussion of the subject and she declined to be drawn into speculation any further.

Dawn came grey and windswept as they climbed beyond the Yorkshire moors to the bleaker and more barren heights of Durham, and then Northumberland, and at last on towards the border with Scotland. They purchased breakfast at one of the many stations, and took it back to eat on the train as it pulled out again.

Vespasia determined not to return to the reason for

their visit, and talked of subjects that might ordinarily have aroused their interest: fashion, theatre, gossip, political events. Neither of them cared just now, but Isobel joined in the fiction that everything was as usual.

As they crossed the Lowlands towards Edinburgh, the brooding and magnificent city that was Scotland's capital and seat of power and learning, the skies cleared, and it was merely briskly cold. The two women alighted and, with the help of a porter, took their luggage to await the train for the last hundred and fifty miles to Inverness.

An hour and a half later they were aboard, stiff, cold and extremely tired, but again moving northwards. As they came into Stirlingshire there was snow on the hills, but the black crown of Stirling Castle stood out against a blue sky with wind-ragged clouds streaming across it like banners.

The country grew wilder. The slopes were black with faded heather and the peaks higher and brilliant white against the sky. On the lower slopes they saw herds of red deer, and once what looked like an eagle, a dark spot circling in the sky, but it could have been a buzzard. The winter afternoon was fading when at last they pulled into Inverness and saw the sprawl of sunset fire across the south, its light reflected paler on the sea. The mound of the Black Isle lay to the north and, beyond that, the snow-gleaming mountains of Ross-shire and Sutherland.

The wind on the platform was like a scythe, cutting through even the best woollen clothing, and there was the smell of snow in it, and vast, clean spaces. It was an unconscious decision to find lodgings for the night rather than make any attempt to find Mrs Naylor's house in the dark, in a town with which neither of them had the slightest familiarity. The station hotel seemed to offer excellent rooms, and had two available. The morning was soon enough to face the ultimate test.

Enquiry of the staff of the hotel elicited the information that the address on Gwendolen's letter was not actually in Inverness itself but was a considerable estate on the outskirts of Muir of Ord, a town some distance away, for which it would be necessary to hire a trap, and it would take a good part of the morning to reach it.

Thus it was close to midday when Vespasia and Isobel finally reached the Naylor house, set in several acres of richly wooded land sweeping down to the Beauly Firth, and ultimately the open sea.

Vespasia looked at Isobel. 'Are you ready?' she asked gently.

'No, nor will I ever be,' Isobel responded. 'But then I am so cold I am not even sure if I can stand on my feet, and whatever lies within that house, it cannot be less comfortable than sitting out here.'

Vespasia wished profoundly that that would prove to be true, but she did not say so aloud.

They alighted, thanked the driver and asked him to wait in case they should not be invited to remain, and have no way of returning to the town. Vespasia hung back

61

and allowed Isobel to step forward and pull the bell knob beside the door. She was about to reach for it a second time, impatient to get the ordeal over, when it swung open and an elderly manservant looked at her enquiringly.

'Good morning,' Isobel said, her voice catching with nervousness now that the moment was upon her. 'My name is Isobel Alvie. I have come from London with a letter of importance to give to Mrs Naylor. With me is my friend Lady Vespasia Cumming-Gould. I would be most grateful if you could give Mrs Naylor that message, and apologise for my not having sent my card first, but the journey is urgent and was unexpected.' She offered him her card now.

'If you will come in, Mrs Alvie, Lady Vespasia, I shall consider what is best to do,' the man said in a soft northern accent.

Isobel hesitated. 'What is best to do?' she repeated.

'Aye, madam. Mrs Naylor is not at home, but I am sure she would wish you to receive the hospitality of the house. Please come in.' He held the door wide for them.

Isobel glanced at Vespasia, then with a shrug so slight it was barely visible, she followed the manservant over the step and inside. Vespasia went after her into a large low-beamed hall with a fire blazing in an open hearth, then past it and into an informal sitting room with sunlight vivid through windows. A lawn sloped downward to a magnificent view beyond, but the room was distinctly cooler than the hall.

'When do you expect Mrs Naylor home?' Isobel

enquired. Her voice was rough-edged and Vespasia could hear the tension in it.

'I'm sorry, madam, but I have no idea,' the man said gravely. 'I'm sorry you've travelled all this way and we cannot help you.'

'Where has she gone?' Isobel asked. 'You must know!'

He looked startled at her persistence. It was discourteous, to say the least.

Vespasia stepped forward. She was not completing the task for Isobel, only ensuring that she had the opportunity to do it for herself. 'I apologise if we seem intrusive,' she said gently. 'But there has been a tragedy in London, and it concerns Mrs Naylor's daughter. We have to bring her news of it, no matter how difficult that may be. Please understand our distress, and concern.'

'Miss Gwendolen?' The man's face pinched with some emotion of pain, but it was impossible to read in it more than that. 'Poor bairn,' he said sadly. 'Poor bairn.'

'We must tell Mrs Naylor,' Vespasia said again, 'and deliver the letter into her hands. It is a duty we have given our word to complete.'

The man shook his head. 'It's no' another death, is it?' he asked, looking from one to the other of them, and back again.

Vespasia allowed Isobel to answer.

'Yes, I am terribly sorry to tell you, it is. So you see why we must speak to Mrs Naylor in person. We were both there, and can at least tell her something of it, if she should wish to know.'

'It'll be Miss Gwendolen herself this time,' he said, shaking his head stiffly, his eyes bright and far distant.

Vespasia felt intrusive in his shock and sadness.

'Yes. I'm profoundly sorry,' Isobel answered. 'Where can we find her, or send a message so she may return, if that is what she would prefer? We are prepared to accompany her south, if she would permit us to.'

'Aye, mebbe.' The servant nodded awkwardly. 'Mebbe. It's a long journey, and that's the truth.'

'Yes it is, but the train transfer in Edinburgh is not too inconvenient.'

'Oh, lassie, there's no train from Ballachulish, and no likely to be in your lifetime, or your grandbairns' neither,' he said with a sad little smile. 'An' maybe that's for the best too. Boat to Glasgow, it'll be. I've heard tell there's railways to Glasgow now.' He spoke of it with an expression as if it were some exotic and far-distant Babylon.

'Ballachulish?' Isobel repeated uncertainly. 'Where is that? How does one get there?'

'Oh, to Inverness, it'll be,' he replied. 'And then down the loch to the Caledonian Canal, and maybe Fort William. Or else across Rannoch Moor and through Glencoe. Ballachulish lies at the end of it, so I'm told.'

'How far is it?' Isobel obviously had no idea at all.

'Lassie, it's the other side o' Scotland! On the west coast, it is.'

Isobel took a deep breath. 'When will Mrs Naylor be back?'

'That's it, you see,' he said, shaking his head. 'She

won't, least not so far as we know. It might be next spring, or then again it might not.'

Isobel was horrified. 'Next spring? But that's . . . that's the other side of winter!'

'Aye, so it is. You're welcome to stay the night, while you think on it,' he offered. 'There's plenty of room. There's been barely a soul in the house since poor Mr Kilmuir met his accident. It'll be good to have someone to cook for, and the sound of voices not our own.'

'Has Mrs Naylor been gone so long?' Vespasia put in with surprise. 'I thought that was well over a year ago?'

'Year and a half,' he replied. 'Early summer, it was, of 'fifty-one. Now if I can get you some luncheon, perhaps . . .? You'll not have eaten, I'll be bound.'

'Thank you,' Vespasia accepted before Isobel could demur. They needed sustenance, and even more they needed the time it would take in order to make a decision in the face of this devastating news.

'What on earth are we going to do?' Isobel asked as soon as they were alone in the main hall again where the fire was warmer. 'Will they listen if I explain to them that Mrs Naylor wasn't here, and wherever she is is at the other side of Scotland, and there's no way to get there?'

'No,' Vespasia said frankly. 'For a start, if she is there, then there must be a way for us to get there also.' But as she said it she felt panic well up inside her. She had spoken on impulse when she promised to come as far as Inverness with Isobel. Part of it was sympathy, part a profound and increasing dislike for Lady Warburton and a desire to see her thwarted and, a good deal more than she had realised before, a desire for Omegus' respect, even admiration. Now the task was beginning to look far greater than she had bargained for. But pride would not let her falter now, and honesty would not allow her to let Isobel believe that what they had done so far would satisfy their oath.

Isobel stared into the fire, her face set, jaw tight. 'This is ridiculous! Why on earth did this wretched woman go across to the other side of the country? How did Gwendolen suppose anyone was going to get a letter to her? Nobody thought about that when they sent us on a wild-goose chase all the way up here!'

It was an implied criticism of Omegus, and Vespasia found it stung.

'Nobody sent us here,' she replied. 'It was an opportunity offered so you could redeem yourself from a stupid and cruel remark which ended in tragedy. Omegus did not cause any part of that.'

Isobel swung round in her chair. 'If Gwendolen had any courage at all she would simply have answered me back, not gone off and thrown herself into the lake! Or if she wanted to make a grand gesture, then she could at least have done it in the daytime, when someone would have seen her and pulled her out!'

'Sodden wet, her clothes clinging to her, her hair like rats' tails, covered in mud and weed? To do what, for heaven's sake?' Vespasia asked. 'It may be romantic to fling yourself into the lake. It is merely ridiculous to be dragged out of it!' But as she stood up and walked away from Isobel towards the window looking over the long slope towards the sea, other thoughts stirred in her mind, memories of Gwendolen happy and with ever-growing confidence. Deliberately she then pictured the moment Isobel had spoken, the freezing seconds before anything had changed, and then Gwendolen's face stricken with horror. She did not understand it. It was out of proportion to the cruelty of the words. It must have been the fact that Bertie did not defend her, and then later did not even go after her to protest his disbelief of anything so shallow in her that had hurt her more than she could bear. It was the wound of disillusion. Perhaps she really had loved him, and not seen his reality before.

She tried to recall Gwendolen all through the Season. Had she really seemed so fragile? Image after image came to her mind. They were all ordinary: a young woman emerging from mourning, beginning to enjoy herself again, laughing, flirting a little, being careful with expenses, but not seemingly in any difficulty. But had Vespasia looked at her more than superficially?

For that matter had she looked at Isobel more than as an intelligent companion, a little different from the ordinary, with whom it was agreeable to spend time, because she had opinions and did not merely say what was expected of her? Vespasia had not honestly sought anything more from her than a relief from tedium. She had told her nothing of herself, certainly nothing of Rome. But she had told nobody of that.

How odd that Mrs Naylor had left here so soon after

Kilmuir's death, and apparently with no intention of returning. Something must have prompted such an extraordinary decision.

She turned and walked out of the hall into the corridor and along to the doorway at the end, which opened on to a gravel path. It was a bright day with a chill wind blowing off the water. The garden was beautifully kept, grass smooth as a bowling green, perennial flowers clipped back, fruit trees carefully espaliered against the south-facing walls. She walked until she found a man coming from the kitchen garden, introduced herself and complimented him on it. He thanked her solemnly.

'Mrs Naylor must miss this very much,' she said conversationally. 'Is Ballachulish equally pleasant?'

'Och, it's very grand, and all that, with the mountains and the glen, and so on,' he answered. 'But the west is too wet for my liking. It's a land full of moods. Very dramatic. No much use for growing a garden like this.'

'Why would one choose to live there?' How bold dare she be?

'There you have me, my lady,' he confessed. 'I couldn't do it, and that's the truth. But if you're a west-coaster it's different. They love it like it was woven into their skins.'

'Oh? Mrs Naylor is a west-coaster?' How simple after all.

'Not she! She's an Englishwoman like yourself,' he said as if it surprised him too. 'She just took up and went there after poor Mr Kilmuir was killed. Took it terrible hard. Mind, it was a bad thing, and so sudden, poor man.'

'Yes, indeed,' she said sympathetically, shivering a little as the wind knifed in over the water, ruffled and white-crested now. 'Although I never heard exactly what happened. Poor Gwendolen was too shocked to speak of it.'

'Horse bolted,' he said, lowering his voice. 'Kilmuir and Mrs Naylor were out in the trap. He was thrown over by a branch, and got himself caught in the rein by his wrist.'

'He was dragged?' she said in horror. 'How appalling! No wonder Gwendolen could not speak of it! Poor Mrs Naylor. She must have been frightened half out of her wits!'

'Och, no, my lady, not she!' he said briskly, dismissing the very idea. 'You do not know Mrs Naylor if you would think that! More courage than any man I know! Any two men!' He lifted his head with fierce pride as he said it. He looked at her through furrowed brows. 'You can smile, but it's true! Stopped the horse herself, but too late to help him, of course. Must have gone in the first moments. Cut the animal free and rode it home to tell us. Clear as day it was, when we found the wreckage, and poor Kilmuir.'

'And Mrs Kilmuir?' Vespasia asked.

He shook his head. 'That's the worst of it, madam. She was out riding, and she saw the whole thing, but too far away to do anything but watch, like seeing your life coming to an end in front of your eyes.' He shook his head minutely. 'Didn't think she'd ever be the same again, poor child. Inconsolable, she was. Wandered around like a ghost, didn't eat a morsel, nor say a word to anyone. Glad we were when she finally went back to London, and word came that she'd started her life again, the poor lass.'

'And Mrs Naylor didn't go with her?'

His face stiffened and something within him closed. 'No. She's no fondness for London, and too much to do up here. And if you'll be excusing me, my lady, I have to take these in for Cook to prepare dinner, since you and your friend will be staying. We'd like to treat you to our best, seeing as you're friends of Mrs Kilmuir's. Walk in the garden all you will, and welcome.'

She thanked him, and continued on, but her mind was lost in picturing the death of Kilmuir, Mrs Naylor's reaction, and her attempts to comfort a shattered daughter who had accidentally witnessed it all. She felt a consuming guilt that now they had to find Mrs Naylor and tell her even worse news. The question of returning to London and simply leaving Gwendolen's letter to be found when she returned, whenever that was, had been irrevocably answered. It was unthinkable.

She told Isobel so when they were alone after dinner.

Isobel turned from the window where she had been standing before the open curtains, staring at the darkness and the water beyond. 'Go down the Caledonian Canal, and then overland to Balla— whatever it is?' she said in anguish. 'How would we do that? Would anyone in their right mind at this time of year? Apart from sheep-herders, and brigands, that is!'

'Well, I shall try it,' Vespasia responded. 'If you wish to go back to London then I am sure they will take you to

Inverness. I shall go on at least as far as I can, and attempt to deliver the letter to Mrs Naylor, and tell her as much as I know of what happened.'

Isobel's face was white, her eyes wide and angry. 'That is moral blackmail!' she accused bitterly. 'You know what they would say if I went back when you went on! It would be even worse for me than if I'd never come!'

'Yes, it probably would,' Vespasia agreed. 'So you will blackmail me into going back and leaving that poor woman to discover that her daughter is dead – whenever she returns here, this year, or next!'

Isobel blinked.

A Christmas Journey (2nd Part)

'We appear to have reached an impasse,' Vespasia observed coolly. 'Perhaps we should both do as we think right? I am going to Ballachulish, or as far towards it as I can. As you may have noticed, there is very little snow so far.'

Isobel bit her lip and turned away. 'You always get what you want, don't you,' she said quietly. Her voice was trembling, but it was impossible to tell if it was from anger or fear. 'You have money, beauty and a title, and, by heaven, do you know how to use them!' And without looking back she swept out of the room and Vespasia heard her steps across the hall.

Vespasia stood alone. Surely what Isobel said was not true? Was she so spoiled, so protected from the reality of other people's lives? Certainly she had great beauty, she could hardly fail to be aware of that. If the looking-glass had not told her, then the envy of women and the adoration of men would have. It was fun – of course it was – but what was it worth? In a few years her beauty would fade, and those who valued her for that alone would leave her for the new beauty of the day, younger, fresher.

And yes, she had money. She admitted she was unfamiliar with want for any material thing. And a title? That too. It opened all manner of doors that would always be closed to others. Was she spoiled? Was she without any true imagination or compassion? Did she lack strength, because she had never been tested?

No, that was not true! Rome had tested her to the last ounce of her strength. Isobel would never know what she would have given to stay there with Mario, whatever their ideological differences: his republicanism and her monarchist loyalty; his revolutionary passion and fire and her belief in treasuring old and beautiful ways that had proved good down the centuries. Over it all towered his laughter, his warmth, his courage to live or die for his beliefs. How unlike the ordinary, pedestrian kindness of her husband, who gave her freedom but left her soul empty.

But that was nothing to do with Isobel, and she would never know of it. This was her journey of expiation, not Vespasia's.

They set out immediately after breakfast, Mrs Naylor's household providing them with transport by pony and trap as far as Inverness, and then beyond to the eastern end of Loch Ness, where they could hire a boat. It would take them the length of the long, winding inland lake with its steep mountain sides as if it were actually a great cleft in the earth filled with fathomless satin-grey water, bright as steel. All the way there they had spoken barely a word to each other, sitting side by side in the trap, the wind in their faces, rugs wrapped tightly around their knees.

'It's a good thirty mile to Fort Augustus, so it is,' the boatman said as they embarked. He shook his head at the thought. 'Then there's the canal, and another good thirty mile o' that, before you reach Fort William on the coast.' He squinted up at the sky. 'And they always say in the west that if you can see the hills, it'll rain as sure as can be.'

'And if you can't?' Isobel asked.

'Then it's raining already,' he smiled.

'Then we'd best get started,' she answered briskly. 'Since it is a fine day now, obviously it is going to rain!'

'Aye,' he acknowledged. 'If that's what you want?'

Without looking at Vespasia, Isobel repeated that it was, and accepted the boatman's assistance into the stern of the small vessel, most of it open to the elements. It was the only way in which they could begin their journey.

They pulled out into the open water, but stayed closer to the northern shore, as if the centre might hold promise of sudden storm, and, indeed, several times squalls appeared out of nowhere. One moment everything was dazzling with silver light on the water, the slopes of the

77

mountains vivid greens. Then out of the air came a darkness, the peaks were shrouded and the distance veiled over with impenetrable sheets of grey, driving rain.

They sheltered in the tiny cabin as the boat rocked and swung, flinging them from side to side. They said nothing, so cold their limbs shook, teeth clenched together.

Vespasia cursed her own pride for coming, and Isobel for her cruel tongue, Omegus for his redeeming ideas, and Gwendolen for wanting a shallow man like Bertie Rosythe, and falling to pieces when she realised what he was.

'Do you suppose Gwendolen was still in love with Kilmuir?' she asked when they finally emerged into a glittering world, the water a flat mirror, burning with light in the centre, mountains dark as basalt above, and drifts of rain obscuring the distance.

Isobel looked at her in surprise. 'You mean she realised it that evening, and the grief of losing him returned to her?' There was a lift of hope in her voice.

'Did you know her, other than just socially during the Season?' Vespasia questioned.

Isobel thought for a few moments. They passed a castle on the foreshore, its outline dramatic against the mountains behind. 'A little,' she answered. 'I know there was a sadness in her under the gaiety on the surface. But then she was a widow. I know what that is like. Whether you loved your husband wildly or not, there is a terrible loneliness at times.'

Vespasia felt a stab of guilt. 'Of course there must be,'

she said gently. It was not Isobel's right to know that it afflicted her also, a different kind of loneliness, a hunger that had never been fed, except in brief, dangerous moments, a shared cause, a time that could never have lasted.

'Actually I thought Kilmuir was a bit of a cad,' Isobel went on thoughtfully. 'I'm not sure that he was any better than Bertie Rosythe, really. But it's natural to remember only what was good about someone after they are dead.'

Vespasia studied her face and saw doubt in it, and something that looked like guilt as Isobel stared across the bright water, with its shifting patterns, and not once after that did she look back at Vespasia, nor raise the subject again.

They stayed the night ashore, and continued the next day, reaching Fort Augustus by evening. They parted from that boat and set out on the canal at sunrise in another. The biting cold, the sense of claustrophobia on the long, narrow boat, and the knowledge that they were moving ever further from land familiar to them, even by repute, eased some of the tension between them. But above all was the dread of meeting Mrs Naylor and having to tell her the truth. They spoke, to break the silence of the vast land and the strangeness of the situation. They sat closer to each other to keep a little warmth, and they shared food when it was offered them, and laughed self-consciously at the inconvenience of the requirements of nature. They filled the long tedium of waiting for locks to fill, or empty, stretching their legs by walking back and forth in the bitter wind, staring at the white-crowned hills.

Some time after dark on the fourth day from Inverness they arrived in Fort William, and again found lodgings. They were shivering with cold and exhaustion, and wretched beyond even thinking of how to move on from there to Ballachulish. They huddled by the fire trying to get warm enough to think of sleep.

'Why, in the name of heaven, would Mrs Naylor come here at all?' Isobel said wretchedly, rubbing her hands together and holding them out from the flames. 'Let alone stay for a year and a half? No wonder Gwendolen never mentioned her. She was probably terrified in case anyone discovered she was insane!'

'Did she never mention her?' Vespasia asked, although Isobel's remark was sensible enough. She had wondered herself why Mrs Naylor was not living in her very attractive house at Muir of Ord. If one wished seclusion, that was surely far enough from Society?

'Never,' Isobel said frankly. 'Which you must admit is unusual.'

A new realisation came to Vespasia. She had not appreciated before that Isobel had known Gwendolen so well that such an omission would be noticeable to her. In fact there was rather a lot that Isobel had not said, but perhaps her own desire for Bertie Rosythe's affection was deeper than it had seemed at Applecross.

'Yes,' Vespasia said aloud. 'Yes, it is.' Actually she wondered why Mrs Naylor had not come to London with

Gwendolen to chaperone her and give all the help she
could in gaining a second husband as soon as it was
decent to do so.

'Exactly.' Isobel tried to move her chair even closer to
the fire, then realised that it would place her feet practi-
cally in the hearth, and her skirts where a spark might
catch them, and changed her mind. 'I'm dreading meeting
this woman.' She looked up at Vespasia candidly. 'Do you
suppose she might actually be dangerous?'

Vespasia weighed in her mind the need to continue their
journey to the end, wherever that might be, and her
growing hunger to know the truth of Gwendolen's reason
for taking her own life. She was becoming concerned that
what they had seen at Applecross was only a small part of
it. The more she considered it, the less did it seem a
sufficient reason.

'I suppose it is possible,' she answered. 'What did
Gwendolen say about her family, if she did not speak of
her mother at all?'

'Very little. It was all Kilmuir, and I suppose even that
was only how much she missed him.' Isobel frowned.
'Naturally she did not speak of the event of his death, but
one would not expect her to. It would have been very poor
taste, distressing for her and embarrassing for everyone
else.' She shivered again and wrapped her cloak more
tightly around her shoulders. 'I have to confess, she
behaved as I think I would have myself in that. I cannot
fault her. It is simply odd that with a mother still living
she never referred to her at all. However, if she's quite

deranged, it would explain it completely.' She puckered her brow. 'Do we really have to continue until we find her?'

'Do you wish to turn back?'

Isobel pulled a rueful little face. 'I wished to turn back as soon as we left Applecross, but not nearly as much as I do now. But I suppose since we have come this far, I should hate to have it all be in vain.' She smiled and her eyes were bright for a second. 'When it gets unbearably cold, miserable and far from anything even remotely like home, I think of how furious Lady Warburton and Blanche Twyford will be if I complete this and they are obliged to forgive me, and it gives me courage to go on.'

Vespasia knew exactly what she meant. The thought of Lady Warburton being charming because she had no choice, and biting back her moral judgements, had warmed her frozen body and put new vigour in her step more than once.

She smiled. 'What was he like, Kilmuir?'

Isobel turned away, a shadow falling between her and Vespasia again as clearly as if it had been visible. 'I don't know.'

'Yes, you do,' Vespasia insisted. 'You knew Gwendolen far longer, and far better, than you have allowed me to suppose.'

Isobel stared at her, her dark eyes wide and challenging. 'If I did, why is that your concern? I am going to do my penance – is that not enough for you? You, of all people, can see what a bitter thing it is!' She took a sudden sharp breath. 'Is that actually why you are here, to make sure I do it all? Is that why Omegus Jones sent you?'

Vespasia was taken aback. The accusation was so unjust it took her completely by surprise. 'I came because I thought the journey could be long and hard, possibly even dangerous, and the ending of it the most difficult of all, and that you might surely need a friend,' she answered. 'Had I been making it, I should not have wished to do it alone. And Omegus did not send me.'

Shame filled Isobel's face. 'I'm sorry,' she said huskily. 'I have not ever been that sort of a friend to anyone. I find it hard to believe you could do it for me. Why should you? I . . . I don't think I would do it for you.' She looked away. 'Not that you would ever need it, of course.'

Vespasia was tempted to answer her with truth, even to tell her some of the weight she carried within her, which was not only loneliness but, if she were honest, guilt as well, and fear. She had buried her memories of Rome, of passion, of the inner joy of not being alone in her dreams. Deliberately she had forced herself not to think of talking with someone who understood her words even before she said them, who filled one hunger even as he awoke others. She had refused to look at remembrance of the exhilaration of fighting with all her time and strength for a cause she believed in. She had returned to duty, to a round of social chitchat about a hundred things that did not matter, and never had. She was now sitting with Isobel, of whom she knew so little, and who knew her even less, sharing the outward hardships of a journey, with an uncrossable gulf between them over the inner purpose of it, that she had no crusade any more. She had no battle to fight except against boredom, and there was no victory at the end of it, only another day to fill with pastimes that nourished nothing inside her.

'You have no idea whether I would or not,' she said quietly. 'You know nothing about me, except what you see on the outside, and that is mostly whatever I wish you to see, as it is with all of us.'

Isobel looked startled. It had never occurred to her that Vespasia was anything more than the perfect beauty she seemed.

The fire was burning low. The wind battered the rain against the glass and whined in the eaves. Unless it eased, the boat journey down the loch to Ballachulish was going to be rough and unpleasant, but at this time of the year it would be days, if not weeks, before there was another fine, still day. Waiting for it was not a choice.

Isobel seemed lost in thought, overcome by new, previously unimagined ideas.

'Why did you say what you did to Gwendolen?' Vespasia asked. 'You half implied that her choice somehow lay between servants and gentlemen, and she chose gentlemen for reasons of money and ambition.'

Isobel blushed. It was visible even in the dying firelight. Several moments passed before she answered, and she did not look at Vespasia even then. 'I know it was cruel,' she said softly. 'I suppose that's why I'm really making this ridiculous journey, otherwise when we got to Inverness and found Mrs Naylor wasn't home, I might have posted the letter, and said I had done my best.' She gave a little shudder. 'No – that's not true, I'm doing it because I know I won't survive in Society if I don't, and I have nowhere else to go, nowhere else I know how to behave, or what to do.'

'The reason?' Vespasia prompted.

Isobel lifted one shoulder in half a shrug. 'Gossip. Stupid, I expect, but I heard it in more than one place.'

Vespasia waited. 'That is only half an answer,' she said at last.

Isobel chewed her lip. 'Everyone turns a blind eye if a man beds a handsome parlour maid or two, as long as he is reasonably discreet about it. A woman who was known to have slept with a footman would be ruined. She would be branded a whore. Her husband would disown her for it, and no one would blame him.'

Vespasia could hardly believe it. 'Are you saying Gwendolen Kilmuir slept with a footman? She must be insane! Far madder than her mother!'

Isobel looked at her at last. 'No, I'm not saying she did, simply that there were rumours. Actually I think Kilmuir started them.' She shut her eyes as if twisted by some deep, internal pain. 'He was paying rather a lot of attention to Dolly Twyford, Fenton's youngest sister.'

'I thought she wasn't married!' Vespasia was incredulous. There was a convention that in certain circles, once one had borne the appropriate children to one's husband, a married woman might then indulge her tastes, and as long as she did not behave with such indiscretion that it could not be overlooked, no one would chastise her for it. However, for a man to have an affair with a single woman was quite another thing. That would ruin her reputation, and make any acceptable marriage impossible for her.

'She wasn't,' Isobel agreed. 'That was the whole point. The suggestion was that Gwendolen's conduct was so outrageous he would divorce her, and then after a suitable period, not very long, he would marry Dolly.'

'Were they in love?'

'With what?' Isobel raised her eyebrows. 'Dolly wanted a position in society, and the title probably coming to Kilmuir, and he wanted children. He had been married to Gwendolen for six years, and there was none so far. He was growing impatient. At least that was the gossip.' Her voice dropped. 'And I knew it.'

Vespasia did not answer. To say that it did not matter would be a dishonesty that would serve no one. Some penance was due for such a cruelty, and they were both deeply aware of it. But more than that, her mind was racing over the new picture of Gwendolen as it emerged now. Had Bertie Rosythe heard the gossip as well, and was that the truth of why he had not gone after her and reassured her of his love? Or worse than that, had he gone, and far from offering her any comfort, had made it plain that he had no intentions towards her? Did she see herself as ruined, not only for him, but for any marriage at all?

Or worse even than that, could such rumours be true? Which raised the bitterly ugly question of whether

Kilmuir's death had been a highly fortunate accident for Gwendolen, releasing her from the possibility of a scandalous divorce from which her reputation would never have recovered. Instead she had become a widow, with everyone's sympathy, and excellent prospects of in time marrying again. How fortunate for her that it had been Mrs Naylor who had been with him in the carriage, and not Gwendolen herself.

They discussed it no more. The fire was fading and sleep beckoned like comforting arms. They were both happy to go upstairs and sink into oblivion until tomorrow morning should require them to face the elements, and attempt to reach Ballachulish.

It was a hard journey, even though not long as the crow, or the gull, were to fly. The sharp west wind obliged the little boat to tack back and forth down the coast through choppy seas, and both Isobel and Vespasia were relieved to put ashore at last in the tiny town of Ballachulish, and feel the earth firm beneath their feet. They crossed the road from the harbour wall, heads down against the sleet, wind gusting, tearing skirts, and made their way to the inn. They asked the landlord about Mrs Naylor, and his response brought them close to despair.

'Och, I'm that sorry to tell ye, but Mistress Naylor left Ballachulish nigh on a year ago!' he told them with chagrin.

'Left?' Isobel could scarcely believe it. 'But she can't!' Her household in Inverness told us she was here!'

'Aye, and so she was,' he agreed, nodding. 'But she left a year ago this Christmas. Grand lady, she was. Never knew any one lady of such spirit, for all that she was as English as you are.'

Isobel swallowed. 'Where did she go? Do you know?'

'Aye, I do. Up through the Glen and over the moor to the Orchy. You'll no' be going that way, though, till May, or so. Even then it's a wild journey. Horses you'll need. The High Road passes right around there, and then south.'

Isobel looked at Vespasia, the first signs of defeat in her eyes.

Vespasia felt a rush of pity, first for Isobel, knowing what awaited her in London if she failed. Her judges would not care what was the reason, or if they could or would have done differently themselves. They were looking for excuses, and any would serve. Then she felt for Mrs Naylor. However mad she was, whatever reason had brought her here and then driven her to go up into Glencoe and beyond, she still deserved to be told about her daughter's death face to face, not in a letter half a year later.

'I accept that it may be difficult,' she said to the landlord. 'Is it possible, with good horses and a guide?'

The man considered for several seconds. 'Aye,' he said at last. 'Ye'll be used to riding, I take it?'

Vespasia looked at Isobel. She had no idea of the answer.

Isobel nodded. 'Certainly. I've ridden in London often enough.'

'Ye'll be needing a guide,' he warned.

'Naturally,' Vespasia agreed. 'Would you arrange one for us, at whatever you consider a fair rate?'

Isobel blinked, but she made no demur.

So it was that the next morning they set out in the company of a grizzled man by the name of MacIan, with a strong Highland pony each to ride, and three more to follow with luggage, water and food.

'Keep close!' MacIan warned, fixing each of them in turn with a sceptical eye. 'I'll no' have time to be nursemaiding ye, so if ye're in trouble, call out, don't just sit there and hope I'll be noticing, 'cause I won't. I've my work to keep these ponies on the track, not to speak of finding it mysel', if the weather turns.' He cocked his head to one side and looked up at the wild sky with clouds racing across it, casting the hills in brilliant light one moment, then shrouded in purple, and then black the next. The water in the lock was white-ruffled. The wind was laden with salt and the sharp smell of weed. It was ice cold on the skin, whipping the blood up.

Isobel looked at Vespasia. For once they understood each other perfectly. Pride kept them from turning back. 'Of course,' they both agreed, and when MacIan was satisfied that they meant it, they set out from the village on the rough road through ever-steepening mountains towards the great glen of the most treacherous massacre in the history of Scotland. In the winter of 1692 the Campbell guests had risen in the night and slain their

MacDonald hosts, man, woman and child – all in the cause of loyalty to the Hanoverian king from the south.

They rode in silence because no conversation was possible. The wind tore their breath away, even had the labour of riding in single file along the track and the grandeur of the scenery not robbed them of the wish to frame words.

At about one o'clock they stopped for something to eat, but primarily to rest the ponies. They were slightly sheltered by a buttress of rock, and Vespasia leaned against it and stared around her. On every side jagged mountains soared into the sky. Some were dark with heather on the lower slopes, the peaks like white teeth in the giant, upturned skull of some vast creature left behind from the beginning of time. The smell of the snow whetted the edge of the wind. It was a land of golden eagles and red deer, pools of peat-dark water, avalanches and blizzards. There was a majesty, a terror, and a beauty that burned itself into the soul.

They remounted and set off again, climbing higher as the valley rose and the sides became steeper yet. Darkness fell early and they stopped at a small hut, almost invisible in the dusk, amid the rock outcrops. It offered little hospitality beyond shelter from the elements, both for them, and for the ponies. Vespasia was glad of that. She would not have left any creature out in the storm that was threatening, let alone beasts upon whom their lives might depend.

'Mrs Naylor must be a raving madwoman,' Isobel said

grimly, settling down to sleep in her clothes. The only concession to comfort was to take the pins out of her hair. 'And I'm beginning to think we are too.'

Vespasia was obliged to agree with her. The longer this journey continued, the more concerned she became as to what manner of woman Mrs Naylor might be, and increasingly now, what had been the truth of the marriage between Gwendolen and Kilmuir, and exactly how he had died. Why had Gwendolen never spoken of her mother? What was the reason for what looked unmistakably like an estrangement?'

Neither of the women slept well. It was too cold and the wooden bunks were hard. It was a relief when daylight came and they could rise, eat a breakfast of porridge and salt and drink hot tea, without milk, then continue on their way.

Outside was a staggeringly new world. It had snowed during the night and the sky had cleared. The light was blinding. Sun glittered on ribbons of water cascading down the rock faces, hitting stones and leaping up, foaming white. An eagle drifted on the wind, a black speck against the blue.

They rode all day, resting only briefly for the ponies' sake. Vespasia was so tired from the unaccustomed exercise that every bone and muscle in her body ached, and she knew Isobel must feel the same, but neither of them would admit it. It was not that they imagined they were deceiving anyone, least of all MacIan, it was simply a matter of self-mastery. One complaint or admission would lead to another, and then perhaps thoughts of surrender. Once suggested it would become a possibility, and that must not be permitted. The temptation was too powerful. Instead they concentrated on a few yards at a time, from here to the next turn in the track, the next stretch ahead.

Then just before dusk, as the sun was setting in shards of fire almost due to the south, the valley opened out and the great width of Rannoch Moor lay in front of them, dark-patched with heather and peat bogs, pools shining bronze in the dying light. In the distance of the sky, turquoise drifted into palest blue before the advancing shades of the night.

No one spoke, but Vespasia wondered if perhaps Mrs Naylor were not so mad after all. This was a different kind of sanity, undreamed of in London.

They found shelter again, but it was bitterly cold, and by morning the aches that had been slight the previous day were now sharper and reminded them of pain with every movement. It required all the concentration Vespasia could muster just to stay on her pony and watch where she was going. Her head ached from clenching her teeth and she was stiff with cold. Not to complain had become a matter of honour, almost a reason for survival.

Clouds appeared on the horizon, billowing, burning with light, as if there had been an explosion just beyond their vision. Then hard on their heels came the squall, driving rain turning to sleet, pellets of ice that stung the skin. They bent into it, heads down, and kept going.

There was nothing to break the strength of it, nothing to hide behind. They moved carefully, one step at a time.

It cleared again just as suddenly and they were able to increase speed.

'We need to be in Glen Orchy by night,' MacIan said grimly. 'There's no place to rest before then, and the Orchy's no river to be stopping near, if ye've no house nor bothy to protect you.'

Vespasia did not bother to ask why not; her imagination supplied a dozen answers. She was beginning to feel as if whatever Mrs Naylor was like, it was going to be a blessed relief to find her and discharge their duty. It could hardly be worse than this. The trek had assumed nightmare properties. Perhaps the Vikings were right and hell was endless cold, a howling wind, a journey that never arrived anywhere, aching bones and muscles, and always the need to press onwards.

Except surely hell could never be so soul-rendingly beautiful?

She noticed Isobel sway in the saddle ahead of her, and more than once she was afraid she would fall herself, but by dusk they saw lights ahead of them. It seemed another endless, excruciating hour before they reached them and found them to be the windows of a large house, far greater in size than that for a single family.

Someone must have seen them come, because the door opened wide as their ponies' hooves clattered in the yard, and a large man with a storm-weathered face stood holding a lantern high.

'Well, MacIan, is it you, then? And what are you doing out on a night like this? Who is it you have with you? Ladies, is it? Well, come on inside. I'll send Andrew and Willie out to tend to your ponies.'

'Aye, Finn, it's a dreech night now,' MacIan agreed cheerfully, climbing out of the saddle in an easy movement and turning back to help first Isobel and then Vespasia to the ground. Vespasia was horrified to discover she could barely stand up, and but for MacIan's hand, she would have staggered and lost her balance.

The door was held wide and two young men passed her, nodding shyly on their way to tend to the animals. Inside was blessedly warm. She was dizzy with relief. It was not until she had taken off her wet outer clothes and dried her face on the clean, rough towel handed her that she turned to see the woman standing in the doorway regarding her with interest. She was tall, easily as tall as Vespasia, with auburn hair wound carelessly on her head, simply as had been convenient. She wore rough wool clothes, quite obviously designed for warmth and convenience of movement. Her face was wide-eyed, intelligent, handsome in a unique and highly individual way. Before she spoke, Vespasia knew that this was Mrs Naylor.

She turned to Isobel, who seemed frozen, as if, now that the moment had come, she could not find the courage. Crossing the moor had cost all she had.

Vespasia stepped forward. 'Mrs Naylor? My name is Vespasia Cumming-Gould.' She indicated Isobel. 'My friend Isobel Alvie. I apologise for arriving without permission at this hour. We had not realised quite what travelling from Inverness would involve.'

'Beatrice Naylor,' the woman answered, a definite smile on her lips. 'No one does, the first time. But it is an experience that remains indelibly in the mind. What brings you to the Orchy in December? It has to be of the utmost importance.'

Vespasia turned to Isobel. They had already set foot through the door. Could they accept this woman's hospitality, even on a night like this, at the end of the earth, by answering her question with a lie?

Isobel's face was flushed from the sudden warmth inside, but white around the eyes and lips. The final moment of testing had come, the last and the greatest, upon which all the rest depended.

Vespasia realised she was holding her breath, her hands clenched at her sides. She could not help. If she did, she would rob Isobel for ever of the chance to earn her redemption.

Mrs Naylor was waiting.

'It is,' Isobel said quietly, her words half swallowed, her voice trembling. 'I have never found anything harder in my life than bringing you the news that your daughter Gwendolen is dead. And I am bitterly ashamed that I contributed to the circumstances which brought it about.' She held out the envelope. 'This is the letter she wrote to you.' Travelling had bent it a little, but the seal was unbroken.

The man who had opened the door to them moved silently to Mrs Naylor and put his arm round her, holding her steady. He did it as naturally as if physical contact between them were understood. There was a great tenderness in his face, but he did not speak.

The silence stretched until the pain in it was a tangible thing in the room.

'I see,' Mrs Naylor said at last. 'How did it happen?' She stared at Isobel with huge, almost unblinking eyes, as if she could read everything that was in her mind and beneath it, in the search for a truth she would rather not look at, even herself.

Isobel struggled to tear her gaze away, and failed. 'At Applecross,' she began, falteringly. 'It was a long weekend house party, rather more of a week. I don't know if . . .'

'I am perfectly acquainted with weekend house parties, Mrs Alvie,' Mrs Naylor said coldly. 'You do not need to explain Society or its customs to me. How did my daughter die, and what cause have you to blame yourself? I might think you spoke only as a manner of expressing your sympathy, but I can see in your face that you are in some very real way responsible.' She looked briefly at Vespasia. 'Does this include you also, Lady Vespasia? Or are you here simply as a chaperone?'

Vespasia was startled that Mrs Naylor knew of her, as the use of her title made clear. 'Mrs Alvie felt the duty to tell you herself, regardless of what the journey involved,' she answered. 'It is not one a friend would permit her to attempt alone.'

'Such loyalty . . .' Mrs Naylor murmured. 'Or do you share the blame?'

'No, she doesn't,' Isobel cut in. 'It was I who made the remark. Lady Vespasia had nothing to do with it.'

Mrs Naylor blinked. 'The remark?'

Finn made a movement to interrupt, but Mrs Naylor held up her hand peremptorily. 'I will hear this! You know me better than to imagine I will faint, or otherwise collapse. Tell me, Mrs Alvie, how did my daughter die?'

Isobel drew a deep, shivering breath. They were all still standing in the big hallway, relieved only of their outer and wettest clothing. No one had yet eaten or drunk a morsel.

'She went out after darkness, when the rest of us had retired, and threw herself from the bridge across the end of the ornamental lake,' Isobel answered. 'We learned of it only the next morning, when it was too late.'

Finn grasped Mrs Naylor by both arms, but she did not stagger, or lean back against him, though her face was ashen white. 'And in what way were you to blame, Mrs Alvie?' she asked.

No one in the room moved. There was to be no mercy.

'We all believed that Bertie Rosythe would propose marriage to her that weekend,' Isobel said hoarsely, her voice a dry rustle in the silence. 'I made a cruel remark to the effect that she would not have loved him had he been penniless, or a servant. I made it from envy, because I also am a widow, and had hoped to remarry, possibly to Bertie.' She took a deliberate, shuddering breath. 'I had no idea it would cause her such distress, but I accept that it did. Apparently he did not go after her to tell her that he knew it was nonsense. I . . . I am deeply ashamed.' She did not look away but remained facing Mrs Naylor.

'You do not need to tell me why you chose that particular barb,' Mrs Naylor said quietly, her voice brittle, every word falling with clarity. 'Your face betrays that you heard the rumours, and knew the weakness in her armour. Please don't let yourself down by denying it.'

The tears stood out in Isobel's eyes. 'I wasn't going to,' she answered. Vespasia wondered if that were true, and was glad it had not been put to the test. She hated standing here helplessly, but to be of any value, this confrontation between Isobel and Mrs Naylor had to play itself out to the bitter end.

'Who else is aware of this?' Mrs Naylor asked.

'No one, so far as I am aware,' Isobel answered. 'Except Lady Vespasia.'

Mrs Naylor turned to Vespasia.

'That is true,' Vespasia told her. 'Mr Omegus Jones arranged that Gwendolen should be buried privately, in the chapel in his grounds, by a minister he knows who would regard her death as an accident. If we brought you the news, in person, those others present at Applecross that weekend are bound by oath to say nothing of what happened which would challenge that account.'

'Really? And why would they do that?' Mrs Naylor asked sceptically. 'Society loves a scandal. Was it a group of saints you had there?' Her voice was hard-edged with grief and past, bitter experience.

'No,' Vespasia answered before Isobel could. She moved a fraction forward towards the centre of the room, commanding Mrs Naylor's attention. 'They were very ordinary, self-regarding, ambitious, fragile people, just like those it seems you already know. They regarded Mrs Alvie as to blame, and were ready to ruin her, with that certain degree of pleasure that comes when you can do so with an excuse of self-righteousness.'

Mrs Naylor's face twisted at the memory, but she did not interrupt. Vespasia had her complete attention. The rest of the room, Finn, the fire crackling in the hearth, the wind beating against the window need not have existed.

'Mr Jones proposed a trial, the verdict of which was to bind us, upon our oath,' Vespasia went on. 'Whoever was found guilty should undertake a journey of expiation, which, if completed, would wash out the sin. If they failed, then everyone else was free to ostracise them completely, to cut them at every opportunity, exclude them from every event, every conversation, as if they had ceased to exist. But if they succeeded, then anyone who referred to the tragedy afterwards, for any reason public or private, should themselves meet with that same ostracism.'

'How very clever,' Mrs Naylor said softly. 'Your Mr Jones is a man of the greatest wisdom. Expiation? I like that word: it conveys far more than punishment, or even repayment. It is a cleansing. Am I bound by this also?' She turned to Isobel, then back to Vespasia.

'You cannot be,' Vespasia answered, seeing the one ghastly flaw in Omegus' plan. 'You were not party to the oath.' She smiled faintly. 'And it does not seem you would be greatly affected if Society did not speak to you. I find it difficult to imagine you would know, let alone care.'

'You are quite right,' Mrs Naylor agreed. 'But this is sufficient explanation for tonight. You have ridden far, and in inclement weather. We have food a-plenty, and room to spare. And your ponies need rest, whether you do or not.' She looked at Isobel. 'It will perhaps be harder for you to accept my hospitality than it will be for me to give it, but there is none other for miles around, so you had best learn to do it. Jean will find you rooms and food. I wish to retire and read my daughter's last letter to me.' And she took Finn's arm and went out, neither of them turning to look behind.

Isobel and Vespasia had no alternative but to follow Jean, a silent, buxom woman, to where she offered them food and rooms for the night.

When they were settled with the luggage placed conveniently for them, Isobel came to Vespasia's door, and accepted instantly the invitation to come in. Her face was pale, her eyes dark-shadowed with misery.

'I'd almost rather sleep on the moor!' she said wretchedly. 'She knows that! What do you think she'll do tomorrow? Can we leave?'

'No. It is part of our oath that we accompany her to London, if she will allow us to,' Vespasia reminded her.

Isobel closed her eyes, her fists clenched by her sides.

100

'I don't think I can! Seven hundred miles, or more, with that woman! That is more punishment than I deserve, Vespasia. I said something stupid, a dozen words, that's all!'

'Cruel,' Vespasia reminded her quietly, then wished she had been less blunt. It was not necessary. Isobel was perfectly aware of her fault. Vespasia had no right to demand proof of it every time. 'And apart from finishing the task,' she said more gently, 'I am not at all sure that we can leave here without Mrs Naylor's assistance. Do you have the faintest idea how to? I don't even know where we are, do you?'

'I must be mad!' Isobel was close to despair. 'You're right. I expect MacIan is on her side, and most certainly Finn is. Who is he, anyway? For that matter, what is this place, and what in the name of heaven is Mrs Naylor doing here? Apart from apparently living in sin!'

Vespasia ignored the jibe. 'I don't know,' she said. 'But it is an interesting question. Why would a wealthy woman in her middle years choose to spend her time not only a great distance from the rest of Society of any sort, but a virtually impossible distance? In fact, why did she not return to London after Kilmuir's death, when Gwendolen did? It would be the most natural thing to do.'

'The only answer is that there was an estrangement,' Isobel answered. 'Perhaps she will not wish to return to London, with us or alone?'

'Sleep on the thought, if you wish,' Vespasia said drily. 'But do not hold it longer than tomorrow morning.' She

gave her a smile with as much warmth in it as she could
find strength for. 'We shall surmise it,' she added. 'Just
think of Lady Warburton's face. She will be fit to spit
teeth.'

Isobel forced herself to smile back, recognising kindness, if no practical help, and bade her good night.

Vespasia meant to consider the puzzling question further
when she was alone, but the bed was warm and soft, and
she sank almost immediately into a nearly dreamless
sleep. When she awoke it was to find Mrs Naylor herself
standing at the foot of the bed with a tray of tea in her
hand. She set it on the table and sat down. It was
apparent that she had no intention of being dismissed
until she was ready to leave. Vespasia might be an earl's
daughter, but Mrs Naylor was on her own territory, and
no one could mistake it.

'Thank you,' Vespasia said as calmly as she was able to.

'Drink it,' Mrs Naylor responded. 'I've had mine.' She
poured it and passed the cup to Vespasia. 'I have read my
daughter's letter. I have no intention of telling either you
or Mrs Alvie what was in it, but I should like you to
answer a few questions before I accompany you south to
pay my respects at the grave.'

Vespasia's response would normally have been anger,
but there was both a gravity and a pain in this woman
that made anything so self-indulgent seem absurd.

'I will tell you what I can,' she said instead, sitting
upright in the bed and sipping her tea. She should have

felt at a disadvantage, dressed as she was in no more than her nightgown, and with her hair around her shoulders, but Mrs Naylor's candour made that irrelevant also.

'What was your real reason for coming here with Mrs Alvie?' Mrs Naylor asked.

Vespasia's ready answer died on her lips. This wild place, where life and death hung on a pony's footstep, a few inches between the sure path and the cliff edge or the freezing, squelching bog, stripped one of the pretensions that meant so much in Society.

'Then I will tell you,' Mrs Naylor answered for her. 'You were afraid she would not make it alone, her courage would fail her and she would take the many excuses to turn back, if not the first, then the second. Why? What does it matter to you if she fails?'

Vespasia thought for only a moment, then she spoke with absolute certainty. 'Omegus Jones spoke of a pilgrimage of expiation in medieval times,' she said. 'Then it was so dangerous that often the traveller did not return, but it was an act of supreme friendship for a companion to go with him or her. It seemed right to me to go, perhaps for my own reasons as well as hers.' Only as she said the words did she realise their truth. She had her own expiation to make – for Rome, for dreams she should not have allowed herself to entertain, journeys of the heart she should not have made.

'I see,' Mrs Naylor said. 'This Mr Jones seems to be a remarkable man.'

'Yes,' Vespasia agreed too quickly and too sincerely.

Mrs Naylor smiled. 'And that also, I think, has some-thing to do with your reason!'

Vespasia found herself blushing, something she had not done in some time. She was accustomed to being in control, of herself, if not always of the situation.

'Those of us who have lived any of our passions have something to expiate,' Mrs Naylor said gently. 'And those who have nothing are the more to be pitied. My father used to say that if you have never made a mistake, then you have probably never made anything at all. Perhaps Mrs Alvie will realise that in time also. I shall return with you tomorrow, when the ponies have had time to rest and to eat. I have my own journey to make. We shall follow the High Road south, to Tyndrum, and Crianlarich, to Loch Lomond, and from there to Glasgow where we can find a train to London. It will take several days. How many will depend upon the weather, but we should be at Applecross before Christmas.' She stood up. 'You may do as you please today, but I would suggest that you do not leave the house. You don't know your way, and the Orchy is a hungry river. It reaches out from its banks and claims many lives.'

'Mrs Naylor?'

She turned. 'Yes?'

'What is it in this place that holds you?' It was an impertinent question, yet she wished to know so intensely that she defied all the rules of courtesy to ask.

'It is a place of rest on my own journey, Lady Vespasia. Perhaps after I have bidden farewell to my daughter, it may even prove to be the end of it. Why or how is not your concern.' She walked to the door, her back ramrod straight, her head high.

Vespasia did not need to be told that the value of Glen Orchy had much to do with Finn, but she was still turning over in her mind the nature of Mrs Naylor's journey. They had been speaking of the road to answer for mistakes, a nicer word than 'sins', but it held more than the suggestion of mere error. They both knew they were speaking not merely of judgement, but of morality.

Vespasia sat in bed sipping her tea and thinking of Kilmuir's terrible death, and the rumours that Isobel had heard, and the gardener's sudden silence at Muir of Ord, and most of all of Gwendolen's face when Isobel had suggested obliquely that she could have been attracted to a footman, had he the social position to offer her.

Was Kilmuir really so desperate for children he would have put Gwendolen away by slandering her so completely that Society would accept his act, and then marrying Dolly Twyford, leaving Gwendolen an outcast, branded a whore?

Her imagination raced. The possibilities were hideous! She thought of her own children, still little, but one day they would grow up, marry suitably, one hoped with love. What would she do if her daughter faced such ruin of her life? She pictured Kilmuir out driving in the carriage with Mrs Naylor, the horse taking fright, Kilmuir overbalancing and falling, his wrists caught in the reins. The answer was there in her mind. She would have seized the chance and pushed him, and whipped up the horses – at least she would have thought of it! Whether she would ever have done it she could not know – please God she would never find out.

Was that what had happened? And Gwendolen had seen it? That was the estrangement between her and her mother? Either she had never realised Kilmuir's plan, or she had refused to believe it? Or perhaps she had willed herself to forget it afterwards, to imagine that somehow he would change his mind, and it would be all right. He would love her again, and deny the rumours. Dolly Twyford would recede into the past. Maybe one day she would even have the longed-for children herself.

And then Mrs Naylor had ruined it! That would be an estrangement sufficient to send Gwendolen to London, and keep her mother in the furthest reaches of Scotland, further even than Muir of Ord. Perhaps only Glen Orchy would answer that guilt, and maybe even the fear of exposure. Who else might know? Only the staff of the house where it had happened, and they would keep silent, if not from loyalty, then at least for lack of proof. But Mrs Naylor would no longer wish to live there.

And if she had not done it, would Kilmuir have gone ahead and first slandered Gwendolen, and then cast her aside, destitute, and with no home, no friends, no reputation, no skills to earn her own way, except to sell her body on the streets or, more probably, to take her life – as in the end she had done?

Was that what she had heard in Isobel's remark – a

beginning of the old accusation again? Was it history repeating itself, and Bertie Rosythe believing, just as Kilmuir had pretended to? That might indeed make her despair, and embrace death of her own choosing before ruin should overtake her. There was no mother to defend her this time.

How desperately alone she must have felt – a second time falsely accused, and no denial would help. How can you deny something that has only been hinted at, never said? Some people might have attacked in return, but where would that end? Almost certainly in a defeat even more painful. This way ended it almost before it began, certainly before any but a handful of people knew of it.

And then the worst possibility of all struck Vespasia. Had Gwendolen believed that Isobel knew Kilmuir's charge, and was very subtly telling her so, and threatening a lifelong blackmail, a cat-and-mouse torture never to end? If that were true, no wonder she had killed herself. The thought was hideous beyond the mind to realise. Could it even be true? Vespasia hated herself that she could even frame the idea – but Isobel's anger, her need came sharply into focus, as if it had been moments ago that Vespasia had seen the look in her eyes, the desperation for her own social position, and safety. Then sanity reasserted itself and she thrust it away. It had been a moment's cruelty, no more.

She rose and dressed at last, weighed down by a sadness, and an overwhelming pity for both Gwendolen and Mrs Naylor. She went downstairs to find breakfast;

107

she knew the wisdom of not attempting anything on an empty stomach, however little she felt like eating.

She found Isobel downstairs, pacing the floor. She turned round the moment she heard Vespasia's footsteps. She was very pale, dark circles around her eyes making her look ill.

'Where have you been?' she demanded.

'I slept late,' Vespasia answered. 'And I did not get up immediately.' That was true as far as it went. She had decided not to tell Isobel of her conversation with Mrs Naylor, and certainly not of the thoughts that had resulted from it. She was ashamed of where it had led her. She liked Isobel, she always had, but perhaps she did not now trust her as deeply as she once had.

'What are we going to do all day?' Isobel pressed. 'What is this place, do you suppose? I have seen all sorts of people here, as if it were a religious retreat.'

'Perhaps it is.' The thought was not absurd. One could hardly retreat further than this.

Vespasia had breakfast of oatmeal porridge, then toast and very sharp, pungent marmalade, which when she enquired she was told was made on the premises. She immediately purchased two jars to take away with her, regardless of the inconvenience of carrying them. One was for herself, the other for Omegus Jones. She knew his tastes; she had watched him at his own table.

The two women spent the day quietly. The house proved indeed to be a form of retreat – not religious, but beyond question spiritual. Mrs Naylor had found a vocation in listening to the troubled, the lonely and the guilty whose fears robbed them of courage, or the hope that battles could be won.

Vespasia found herself wishing they might stay longer, and she forced herself to remember that this was not her calling, certainly not now, when winter was closing in rapidly. They must accompany Mrs Naylor to London, and then return to Applecross to report to Omegus, and to face Lady Warburton and the others, if they were to still their tongues before spring. They would be bound by the silence of expectation only so long.

She saw Finn several times, and observed in him a humour and a great strength of self-understanding, and she perceived without effort why Mrs Naylor found happiness with him. There was a reserve in him so that there would always be thoughts and dreams to surprise.

It was with regret that she and Isobel set out at daybreak the following morning, with Mrs Naylor and MacIan, and a troup of ponies. Finn saw them to the entrance of the yard, standing with the fierce wind blowing his hair and whipping at his coat. Vespasia knew his goodbyes to Mrs Naylor had already been said, and words were an encumbrance to the understanding they shared.

They set off south, away from the glen along the High Road. It was almost seven miles to Tyndrum, and another five or so to Crianlarich. If they pressed on with only such breaks as the horses needed, they might make it by nightfall. On easy roads a carriage would have done it by luncheon, but this was wild country, the peaks snow-covered, and they went in the teeth of a gale with ice on its edge. One good blizzard might end their journey altogether.

But Mrs Naylor did not hesitate. She led the way with MacIan, and left Vespasia and Isobel to keep up the best they could. Their ponies were as good as anyone's, it was a matter of human endurance, and they were half her age. If she ever thought of doubting them, she gave no sign of it.

They plodded silently through a great sweeping wilderness of mountain and sky, sometimes lit by dazzling sun, blinding off the snow slopes above and ahead. Then squalls drove down from nowhere, and they huddled together, backs to the worst of it, until it was past and they would plough forward again.

Vespasia glanced at Isobel, and received a rueful smile in answer. It was as clear as if they had spoken: at least this flesh-withering cold, the slow, uneven progress, the need to guide their ponies with all possible attention, and even the waste of time to get off and walk, knee-deep in fresh snow, skirts sodden to the thighs, made conversation completely impossible. With Gwendolen's death heavy on heart and mind, it was a blessing, however profound the disguise.

It was well past midday when they reached the inn at Tyndrum and the weather was closing in as if it would be all but dark by three.

'We'll no' make Crianlarich the night,' MacIan said,

squinting upwards at the sky. 'It's after one now, an' it's another five hard miles. We'd best rest the ponies an' start fresh in the morning.'

'Surely we can make five miles by dark?' Isobel said urgently. 'We've done most of it already!'

'We've done seven, Mistress Alvie,' MacIan told her dourly. 'Ye mebbe think ye can do the like again, in two hours, but ye're mistaken. An' I'll no have ye drive my ponies to it. Rest while ye can, and be glad of a spot o' warmth.' He looked at Mrs Naylor. 'Take a dram, mistress. I'll care for the beasts. Get ye inside.'

It was what Vespasia also had dreaded – a long afternoon by the fireside with Isobel and Mrs Naylor. The meal was endurable. They were all still numb with cold and glad of any food at all, let alone hot, savoury haggis rich with herbs, offered them in spite of the nearness to Burns Night. It was served with mashed potatoes and sweet turnips, and afterwards flat, unleavened oatcakes and a delicately flavoured cheese covered with oatmeal, called Cabac.

The remnants of the luncheon were finally cleared away and the travellers were left alone in the small sitting room by the fire, peat to replenish it in the hearth, stags' heads on the wall. The silence was leaden, and Vespasia saw the slight smile cross Mrs Naylor's lips. She knew in that instant that she understood exactly what was in Isobel's mind, and Vespasia's, and she was mistress of herself sufficiently to outlast both of them. Grief would wound her, perhaps to the heart, but it would not bend or break

111

her. She would meet them on her own terms.

Twice Isobel began to speak, and then stopped. Finally Mrs Naylor turned to her.

'Is there something you wish to say, Mrs Alvie?'

Isobel shook her head. 'Only that we cannot sit here in silence all afternoon, but I see that we can, if that is what you wish.'

'What would you like to speak about?'

Isobel had no answer.

'Glen Orchy,' Vespasia said suddenly. 'I should like to know about how you found it, and how word travels of what you do there, and who is welcome.'

Mrs Naylor regarded her with a wry humour, the smile all turned inwards, as if facing some moment of decision at last. 'You do not ask what I do there, or why I stay,' she observed. 'Is that because you believe I would not tell you? Or does courtesy suggest it would be intrusive?'

'Both,' Vespasia replied. 'But principally because I believe that I know.'

Isobel looked confused.

Mrs Naylor ignored her. 'Do you indeed?' she said dubiously. 'I think not, but we shall not discuss it. If there is debt between us, and I am not sure that there is, then it is you who owe me.'

'I have children,' Vespasia said gently. She was going to add that she knew the consuming love and need to protect, then she saw the warning in Mrs Naylor's face, the sudden tightening of fear, and she remembered also that Isobel had been widowed before she had had a chance to bear children. So she said nothing, but she knew that she was right, and Mrs Naylor knew it also. For the first time, Vespasia took charge of the conversation. She repeated her questions. Mrs Naylor answered them, and through the darkening afternoon both younger women heard a story of extraordinary courage and strength of will, compassion and determination, but told in a way that made it seem the most natural and ordinary thing, in fact the only possible way to behave.

Finding an empty house falling into dereliction, Mrs Naylor and Finn had built and repaired it, until the house was restored to its earlier comfort. Then, with one guest at a time – the first by chance – it had become a hostelry for wanderers who needed not only shelter from the elements of the Highland winter, but from the harder seasons of life, a time to rest and regain not so much strength as a sense of direction, an understanding of mountains, of paths and, above all, of hope.

When they retired after dinner Isobel followed Vespasia up the stairs, almost on her heels. 'What am I going to do?' she said when they reached the bedroom they were to share. There was a note of desperation in her voice.

'What you have told Omegus that you will do,' Vespasia answered. 'Mrs Naylor won't tell people anything other than whatever you tell them yourself.'

'I don't mean about Gwendolen's death!' Isobel said impatiently. 'I mean about anything! I don't want to marry Bertie Rosythe, even if he offered! Or anyone like him. I should die of loneliness, even if it took me all my life to do it, an inch a day.' Her voice was suddenly harsher, as if the anger ran out of control. 'For heaven's sake, are you really so damnably complacent that you don't even know what I mean? Can't you see anything further than money and fashion, the Season, knowing everyone who matters and having them know you, going to all the right parties?' She flung her hand out stiffly. 'What when the door is closed, and you take off your tiara and the maid hangs up your gown? Who are you then?' Now she was almost weeping. 'What have you? Have you anything at all that matters? Is that what comfort has given you – that you are dead at heart, of self-satisfaction?'

Vespasia saw the contempt in Isobel's eyes, and knew that it had been there dormant for all the time they had known each other. Did she care enough to strip away the armour of her own protection to answer truthfully? If not, then she was denying herself, almost as if she were making it true.

'I have too much pain, and too much hope to be dead,' she replied gravely. 'My best days were not wearing a tiara, or a ball gown. I carried bandages and water, and sometimes even a gun. I wore a plain grey dress that was borrowed, and I stood on the barricades in Rome, and fought for a revolution that failed.' She lowered her voice because the tears choked in her throat. 'And loved a man I shall never see again. You have no right to despise anyone, Isobel, until at least you know who they are. And we will probably none of us ever know anyone sufficiently well for that. Be happy for it. It is not a sweet thing to look down on others, or to feel their inferiority. It's lonely, ugly and wrong.' She took a deep breath. 'Sleep well. We must make Crianlarich at least, by tomorrow evening. I know it's only about five miles, but five miles of storm in these hills may seem more than thirty miles at home. Good night.'

'Good night,' Isobel said gently.

The following day they travelled through glancing blizzards, one of them heavy enough to halt them for over two hours, but they reached Crianlarich before sundown, and the day after as far as the head of Loch Lomond, with Ben Lomond towering white in the distance to the south.

After that they kept close to the water until they were past the Ben itself, and on the morning of the fifth day since leaving Glen Orchy, bade MacIan goodbye, and thanked him heartily. They took the boat to the furthest shore of the loch, little more than twenty miles from Glasgow itself. From there it was a matter of hiring a vehicle of any sort, and driving their own way to the railway station. With a trap and good roads, even if the weather were inclement, it was a journey that could be done in one day.

After breakfast Isobel was assisted in, then Vespasia, leaving Mrs Naylor last. Vespasia had intended it so, knowing that Mrs Naylor was an excellent horsewoman, used to driving. After all, it was she who had gained control of the runaway horse that had killed Kilmuir. Whether it was an accident or not she did not know, nor did she wish to. She herself was a fine rider, but unpractised at managing a carriage horse, which was a different skill entirely.

Mrs Naylor hesitated.

Vespasia wondered if it were memories of Kilmuir's death returning to her: doubt, guilt, horror, regret – even fear that it was having witnessed it from her horse, even a hundred yards away or more, that had made Gwendolen's courage for life so fragile. Did she know that her mother had killed to save her? Was that the burden she finally could not bear?

Mrs Naylor sat in the driving seat and picked up the reins awkwardly. She held them in her hands together, not apart, in order to give her control of the animal.

The ostler showed her how, patiently, and still she looked clumsy. The horse sensed it and shifted, shaking its head.

The truth struck Vespasia like a hammer blow. Mrs Naylor did not know how to drive. It was not she who had held the reins when Kilmuir had fallen, accidentally or otherwise, it was Gwendolen herself! Vespasia had seen her driving in London: she was brilliant at it! And it was Mrs Naylor who had been out riding, and had seen. It made infinitely more sense. She had had to protect her daughter, and Gwendolen, in the shock of it, had allowed herself to forget – to move the blame to a more bearable place.

The truth fell in front of Vespasia's eyes in a perfect pattern. The guilt was for having arranged and permitted a marriage to someone like Kilmuir, not to have judged him more accurately. It was a mother's primary duty towards her daughter, and Mrs Naylor had signally failed. That was why she was prepared to take the burden of guilt now. And Gwendolen had allowed it.

Then in one trivial, cruel remark the fragile new image had been shattered – hope, the shield of forgetting, all gone, and the spectre raised of a lifetime's blackmail from others who knew, or at least guessed part of it.

'I'll drive!' Vespasia said, her voice surprisingly steady. The slight tremor in it could be attributed to the cold. 'Let me. I am not as good as Gwendolen was, but I am perfectly adequate.' She scrambled forward to take Mrs Naylor's place. Their eyes met for a moment, and Mrs Naylor knew that she understood.

Vespasia smiled. It would never be referred to again. Isobel could not afford to – she had her own secrets to keep – and Vespasia had no wish to.

Mrs Naylor handed her the reins, and they began the last part of their journey to Glasgow, before the long train ride to London.

The journey was tedious, as it had been on the way up, but they reached London at last. It was three days before Christmas. The final meeting was to be at Applecross, and Vespasia knew that Omegus Jones would already be there. There seemed little point in remaining in the city, so she invited Mrs Naylor and Isobel to go with her to her own

117

country house, which was within ten miles of Applecross. She was uncertain if Mrs Naylor would wish to accept, and surprised how it pleased her when she did.

After greeting her husband and children, the first thing Vespasia did was to write a letter to Omegus Jones and tell him that they had completed their mission, and it remained only to report that fact to make the oath binding. Then she sealed it and called one of the footmen to ride over and deliver it.

'Shall I wait for an answer, my lady?' he asked.

'Oh, yes! Yes, indeed,' she answered him. 'It is of the utmost importance!'

'Yes, my lady.'

When he returned several hours later and gave her the envelope, she thanked him and tore it open without waiting for him to leave.

My dear Vespasia,

You cannot know how relieved I am to hear that you are safely returned, and that you have accomplished in full all you set out to do. The letter of the law would have sufficed to bind our fellows to silence, but it is the spirit which heals the transgressor, and that is in essence what matters.

I admit I have worried about you, veering from one moment having the utmost faith that you would come to no harm, and the next being plunged into an abyss of fear that some natural disaster might overtake you. Had I known the true extent of your journey to the west, I should not have allowed you to go, and none of this would have succeeded. Perhaps it is good that at times we do not know what lies ahead, or we would not attempt it, and failure would be inevitable.

Naturally you will wish to be with your own family for Christmas Day, but will you bring Isobel and Mrs Naylor to Applecross on Christmas Eve, so we may complete our covenant, and Isobel be free? The others of our party that tragic weekend will be here then.

I await your answer with hope,

Your friend and servant,

Omegus Jones.

She folded it with a smile and placed it in the drawer in her escritoire, which had a lock on it. Then she found Isobel and Mrs Naylor, and gave them Omegus' invitation. The following morning she sent the same footman back with their acceptance.

They set out in the afternoon in order to arrive at Applecross for dinner. The day was crisp and cold, but this far south there was no snow yet, only a taste of frost in the air. By the time they arrived they were shivering, even beneath travelling rugs, and glad to alight and go into the great hall decked with holly and ivy, scarlet ribbons, gold-tipped pine cones and great bowls of fruit.

A huge fir tree stood in the corner, covered with ornaments, candles, chains of bright-coloured paper and small, gaily wrapped gifts, its sharp woody aroma filling the air, along with the scent of spices, woodsmoke, and very faintly, the promise of roasted Christmas dinner and hot plum pudding. There was excitement in the whisper of maids' voices, the giggles and the quick rustle of skirts. The fire blazed in the hearth, burning half a log. Footmen met them with glasses of mulled wine and marzipan sweetmeats, warm mince pies and candied peel.

Omegus was delighted to see them. He complimented Isobel, offered his deepest sympathies to Mrs Naylor and said he would tell her all she wished to know when she felt ready to ask, and would take her to the grave at her convenience.

She thanked him, and said that festivities of the season must come first. It was a brave and generous thing to do, and exactly what Vespasia would have expected of her.

Ten minutes later, when the others had gone, Omegus took Vespasia's arm and held her with a startlingly firm grip when she made to move away. 'I think you have more to tell me,' he said quietly.

She swivelled to face him. 'More?'

He smiled very slightly. 'I know you, my dear,' he told her. 'You would not like Mrs Naylor, as I see you obviously do, unless you had come to know her more than superficially. You have learned something of her which has moved you to admiration, something you do not give lightly. The same emotion is not in Isobel, so it seems likely to me that you have not confided it in her. I wonder why not, and the answer is possibly to do with

Gwendolen's death. Is it something I should know?'

Vespasia found herself blushing. She had not intended to tell him, and now she found she could not lie. It was not that she had not the imagination – it would have been simple enough – but she would lose something she valued intensely were she to place that barrier between them.

In a low, very soft voice, she told him what she had guessed, and deduced, of the truth of Kilmuir's death.

'And you did not tell Isobel?' he asked gravely.

'No. It . . .' She saw in his eyes the criticism that was unspoken inside herself. 'She has a right to know – doesn't she?' she finished.

'Yes.' There was no equivocation in him.

'I shall tell her after dinner,' she promised. 'After she has made peace with Lady Warburton.'

His eyebrows rose in question. 'Do you not trust her to keep the same silence for others that she wishes kept for herself?'

Again Vespasia felt the heat burn up her cheeks. 'I'm not sure,' she confessed. 'Mrs Naylor deserves that silence, and Gwendolen needs it. There is no oath to bind her for that.'

He put his hand over hers for an instant, then offered her his arm.

'Shall we go in to dinner?'

The meal was rich and excellent. After the main courses were finished, and long before anyone could think of the ladies withdrawing, Omegus rose to his feet, and the talk ceased.

'My friends, we are met together this Christmas Eve in order to keep an oath that we made less than a month ago. We promised then that if Isobel Alvie were to travel to Scotland and find Gwendolen's mother, Mrs Naylor, and give her Gwendolen's last letter and, should Mrs Naylor be willing, accompanying her back here, then we would wipe from our memory all knowledge of her remarks to Gwendolen on the night of her death. Her part of that oath has been fulfilled . . .'

'You expect us to take her word for that?' Fenton Twyford asked, his face twisted in sarcasm.

'Mrs Naylor is here,' Omegus answered him. 'If you have doubts of Isobel, or of me, then you may ask her.' He indicated Mrs Naylor, where she sat calm and dignified at the table.

Fenton Twyford turned to her, and met an icy stare, and changed his mind. Then he became aware of his impertinence, and blushed.

The flicker of a smile crossed Omegus' face. 'It is now up to us to keep our part. Any man or woman who breaks the promise will cease to be known by the rest of us. We will not speak to them again, invite them to any event public or private, or in any way acknowledge their presence. They will have chosen to be a person whose honour is worthless. I cannot imagine anyone wishes to be such a . . . a creature. Mrs Naylor has promised to be bound by the same code.' He turned to her.

'I have,' she said clearly. 'And I wish to add to that what Mr Jones does not know. Mrs Alvie's part in my daughter's death was smaller than you or she are aware. It was simply the last straw added to a weight Gwendolen was already bearing, placed there by others, of which Mrs Alvie had only a slight knowledge. I have no intention of telling you what burdens those were. It is better buried with her. Sufficient to say that it would be unjust for Mrs Alvie to suffer more blame than she has – and which she has washed away by her acts towards me. It is over.'

Isobel turned to her, her eyes wide, her lips parted in astonishment, and dawning anger. 'You mean they were going to punish me – and I was only partly guilty?'

'Yes,' Mrs Naylor agreed.

Isobel swung round to stare at Lady Warburton. 'You would have ruined me, driven me into a wilderness from which I would never recover! And I wasn't even guilty! Not entirely . . .'

Lady Warburton quaked. 'I didn't know,' she protested. 'I thought you were.'

'You thought so yourself,' Blanche Twyford added. 'You didn't deny it!'

'Yes, I did!' Isobel spat at her. 'You gave no mercy.'

'That is true,' Omegus cut across her, his voice clear and insistent, undeniable. 'And mercy, the gift to forgive, to wash away from the memory as if it had not happened, to accept the gift of God which is love and hope, courage to begin again in the faith that redemption is come into the world, is the meaning of Christmas. That is why we are met here today. It is why we deck the halls with holly, why the bells will ring tonight from village to village across the land until the earth and the sky are filled with their sound.' He turned to Isobel, waiting for her answer, not in words on her lips, but in her eyes.

She hesitated only a moment. 'Of course,' she answered softly. 'I have made my journey and arrived at Christmas, perhaps only at this moment. I shall be grateful all my life that you offered it to me, and to Vespasia for coming with me, when she had no need. How could I accept it for myself, and deny it to another?'

'It is everyone's journey,' Omegus said with a smile of utter sweetness. 'No man needs to make it alone. But his choice to go with another is the one act of friendship which brings us closest to the Man who was born on the first Christmas, and is the Gift of them all.' He raised his glass. 'To the friendship which never fades!'

All around the table the answering glasses were lifted.

Headline hopes you enjoyed reading Anne Perry's A CHRISTMAS JOURNEY and invites you to sample the first chapter of SEVEN DIALS, out now in Headline paperback . . .

Chapter One

Pitt opened his eyes but the thumping did not stop. The first grey of daylight showed through the curtains. Early September, it was not yet six, and there was someone at the front door.

Beside him Charlotte stirred a little in her sleep. In a moment the noise would waken her too.

He slid out of bed and moved quickly across the floor and on to the landing. He ran down the stairs in his bare feet, snatched his coat off the rack in the hall, and with one arm through the sleeve, unbolted the front door.

'Good morning, sir,' Jesmond said apologetically, his hand still in the air to knock again. He was about twenty-four, seconded from one of the local London police stations to Special Branch, and he considered it to be a great promotion. 'Sorry, sir,' he went on. 'But Mr Narraway wants you, straight away, like.'

Pitt saw the waiting hansom just beyond him, the horse fidgeting a little, its breath hanging vapour in the air. 'All right,' he said with irritation. It was not a particularly interesting case he was on, but he had it nearly solved; only one or two small pieces remained. He did not want a distraction now. 'Come in.' He gestured behind him towards the passage to the kitchen. 'If you know how, you can riddle the stove and put the kettle on.'

'No time, sir, beggin' your pardon,' Jesmond said grimly. 'Can't tell you wot it's about, but Mr Narraway said ter come right away.' He stood firmly on the pavement as if remaining rooted to the spot were going to make Pitt return even sooner.

Pitt sighed and went back in, closing the door to keep the damp air out. He climbed the stairs, already taking his coat off, and by the time he was in the bedroom pouring water out of the ewer into the basin, Charlotte was sitting up in bed, pushing her heavy hair out of her eyes.

'What is it?' she asked, although after more than ten years of marriage to him, first when he was in the police, now the last few months in the Special Branch, she knew. She started to get out of bed.

'Don't,' he said quickly. 'There's no point.'

'I'll get you a cup of tea, at least,' she replied, ignoring him and standing on the rug beside the bed. 'And some hot water to shave. It'll only take twenty minutes or so.'

He put down the ewer and went over to her, touching her gently. 'I'd have had the constable do it, if there were time. There isn't. You might as well go back to sleep . . .

128

and keep warm.' He slid his arms around her, holding her close to him. He kissed her, and then again. Then he returned to the basin of cold water and began to wash, ready to report to Victor Narraway – as far as he knew, the head of the Secret Service in Queen Victoria's vast empire. If there were anybody above him, Pitt did not know of it.

Outside the streets were barely stirring. It was too early for cooks and parlour maids, but tweenies, bootboys and footmen were about, carrying in fresh coal, taking deliveries of fish, vegetables, fruit, and poultry. Areaway doors were open and sculleries showed brightly lit in the shadows of the widening dawn.

It was not very far from Keppel Street where Pitt lived, in a modest but very respectable part of Bloomsbury, to the discreet house where Narraway currently had his offices, but it was already daylight when he went in and up the stairs. Jesmond remained below. He had apparently finished his task.

Narraway was sitting in the big armchair he seemed to take with him from one house to another. He was not a large man, slender, wiry, at least three inches shorter than Pitt. He had very thick dark hair, touched with grey at the temples, and eyes so dark they seemed black. He did not apologise for getting Pitt out of bed, as Cornwallis, Pitt's superior in the police, would have done.

'There's been a murder at Eden Lodge,' he said quietly. His voice was low and very precise, his diction perfect. 'This would be of no concern to us, except that the dead man is a junior diplomat, of no particular distinction, but he was shot in the garden of the Egyptian mistress of a senior cabinet minister, and it seems the minister was unfortunately present at the time.' He stared levelly at Pitt.

Pitt took a deep breath. 'Who shot him?' he asked.

Narraway's eyes did not blink. 'That is what I wish you to find out, but so far it looks unfortunately as if Mr Ryerson is involved, since the police do not seem to have found anyone else on the premises, apart from the usual domestic servants, who were in bed. And rather worse than that, the police arrived to find the woman actually attempting to dispose of the body.'

'Very embarrassing,' Pitt agreed drily. 'But I don't see what we can do about it. If the Egyptian woman shot him, diplomatic immunity doesn't stretch to cover murder, does it? Either way, we cannot affect it.' He would like to have added that he had no desire or intention of covering up the fact that a cabinet minister had been present, but he very much feared that that was exactly what Narraway was going to ask him to do – for some perceived greater good of the Government, or the safety of some diplomatic negotiation. There were aspects of being in Special Branch that Pitt disliked intensely, but ever since the business in Whitechapel he had had little choice. He had been dismissed from his position as head of the Bow Street Station, and had accepted secondment to Special Branch as both protection for himself from the persecution that had followed his exposure of the Inner

Circle's power and its crimes. It was also the only avenue open to him to use his skills to earn a living for himself and his family.

Narraway gave a very slight smile, no more than an acknowledgement of a certain irony.

'Just go and find out, Pitt. She's been taken to the Edgware Road Police Station. The house is on Connaught Square, apparently. Somebody is spending a good deal of money on it.'

Pitt gritted his teeth. 'Mr Ryerson, I presume, if she is his mistress. I suppose you are not saying that loosely?'

Narraway sighed. 'Go and find out, Pitt. We need the truth before we can do anything about it. Stop weighing it and judging, and go and do your job.'

'Yes, sir,' Pitt said tartly, standing a little straighter for an instant before turning on his heel and going out, thrusting his hands into his jacket pockets and pushing it out of shape.

He set out along the street westward towards Hyde Park and the Edgware Road, intending to pick up a hansom as soon as he saw one.

There were more people around now, more traffic in the streets. He passed a newsboy with the earliest edition headlining the threat of strikes in the cotton mills of Manchester. The unrest had been grumbling on for a while, and looked like getting worse. Cotton was the biggest industry in the whole of the North-West and tens of thousands of people made their living from it, one way or another. The raw cotton was imported from

Egypt and woven, dyed and manufactured into goods here, then sold again all over the world. The damage of a strike would spread wide and deep.

There was a woman on the corner of the street selling hot coffee. The sky was calm and still, shredded with ragged clouds, but Pitt was chilled enough to find it welcome. There could well be no time for breakfast. He stopped.

'Mornin', sir,' she said cheerfully, grinning to show two missing teeth. 'Lovely day, sir. But a nip in the air, eh? 'Ow abaht an 'ot cup ter start the mornin'?'

'Yes, please.'

'That'll be tuppence, sir.' She held out a gnarled hand, fingers dark with the stain of the beans.

He gave the money to her, and accepted the hot drink in return, then stood drinking it slowly so as not to burn himself, and thinking how he could approach the police when he reached the Edgware Road Station. They would resent his interference. He knew how he had felt when he was in charge of Bow Street. Good or bad, he wanted to handle cases himself, not have his judgement overridden by senior officers who knew less of the area, of the details of the evidence, and who had not even met the people concerned, let alone questioned them.

The cases he had handled so far in Special Branch were largely preventative: matters of finding men likely to cause trouble, violence, intimidation, stirring up the cold, hungry, and impoverished into riot. Occasionally it had been the search for an anarchist or potential bomber. The

Special Branch had been formed originally to combat the Irish Problem, and had had a certain degree of success, at least in keeping violence under control. Now its remit was against any threat to the security of the country, so possibly the fall of a major government figure could be scraped into that category.

He finished the coffee and handed the mug back to the woman, thanking her and continuing along the pavement. He took the last few yards at a run as he saw an empty hansom stop at the intersection, and he hailed the driver.

At the Edgware Road Station an Inspector Talbot was in charge of the case and received Pitt in his office with barely concealed impatience. He was a man of middle height, lean as a whippet, with sad, slightly faded blue eyes. He stood behind his desk, piled with neatly hand-written reports, and stared at Pitt, waiting for him to speak.

'Thomas Pitt from Special Branch,' Pitt introduced himself, offering his card to prove his identity.

Talbot's face tightened, but he waved a hand for Pitt to sit down in one of the rigid, hard-backed chairs. 'It's a clean case,' he said flatly. 'The evidence is pretty hard to misunderstand. The woman was found with the body, trying to move it. It was her gun that shot him and it was in the barrow beside the body. Thanks to someone's quick thought, we got her in the act.' The expression on his face was a challenge, daring Pitt to contradict such blatant facts.

'Whose quickness?' Pitt asked, but his stomach knotted

up with foreknowledge of a kind of hopelessness already. This was going to be simple, ordinary and ugly, and, as Talbot said, there was no way of evading it.

'Don't know,' Talbot replied. 'Someone raised the alarm. Heard the shots, they said.'

'Raised the alarm how?' Pitt asked, a tiny prickle of curiosity awakened in him.

'Telephone,' Talbot answered, catching Pitt's meaning instantly. 'Narrows it down a bit, doesn't it? Before you ask, we don't know who. Wouldn't give a name, and apart from that, they were so alarmed their voice was hoarse, and so up and down the operator couldn't even say for sure whether it was a man or a woman.'

'So they were close enough to be certain it was shots,' Pitt concluded immediately. 'How many houses have telephones within a hundred yards of Eden Lodge?'

Talbot pulled his mouth into a grimace. 'Quite a few. Within a hundred and fifty yards, then probably fifteen or twenty. It's a very nice area, lot of money. We'll try asking, of course, but the fact the person didn't give their name means they want to keep well out of it.' He shrugged. 'Pity. Might have seen something, but I suppose more likely they didn't. Body was found in the garden, well concealed by shrubbery, all leaves still on the trees, barely beginning to turn colour. Laurels and stuff on the ground, evergreens.'

'But you found it straight away?' Pitt pointed out.

'Could hardly miss it,' Talbot said ruefully. 'She was standing there in a white dress, with the dead man draped over a wheelbarrow in front of her, as if she'd just dropped the handles when she heard the constable coming.'

Pitt tried to picture it in his imagination: the dense blackness of the garden in the middle of the night, the crowding leaves, the damp earth, a woman in an evening gown with a corpse in a wheelbarrow.

'There's nothing for you to do,' Talbot interrupted.

'Possibly.' Pitt refused to be dismissed. 'You said there was a gun?'

'Yes. She admitted it was her gun. Had more sense than to try to deny it. Handsome thing, engraved handle. Still warm, and smelled of powder. There's no doubt it was what killed him.'

'Could it have been an accident?' Pitt asked without any real hope.

Talbot gave a little grunt. 'At twenty yards, possibly, but he was shot within a few feet. And what would a woman like that be doing out in the garden with a gun at three in the morning, except on purpose?'

'Was he shot outside?' Pitt asked quickly. Was Talbot making assumptions, possibly wrong?

Talbot smiled very slightly, only a twitch of the lips. 'Either that, or he was left lying outside for some time afterwards; there was blood on the ground. And none inside, by the way.' His expression tightened, his eyes bright and pale. 'Takes a lot of explaining, doesn't it?'

Pitt said nothing. What on earth did Narraway expect him to do? If Ryerson's mistress had shot this man, there

135

was no reason why Special Branch should even think of protecting her, much less lie to do it.

'Who was he?' he said aloud.

Talbot leaned back against the wall. 'I was wondering when you'd ask that. Edwin Lovat, ex-army lieutenant and minor diplomat with an apparently good record behind him and, until last night, a promising future ahead. Good family, no enemies that we've found so far, no debts that we know of yet.' He stopped, waiting for Pitt to ask the next question.

Pitt concealed his irritation. 'So why should this Egyptian woman shoot him, in or out of her house? I assume there was no question of him trying to break in?'

Talbot's eyebrows shot up, wrinkling his forehead. 'Why on earth should he do that?'

'I've no idea,' Pitt replied tersely. 'Why should she be outside in the garden with a gun? None of it makes any sense!'

'Oh, yes it does!' Talbot retorted fiercely, sitting forward and putting his elbows on the desk. 'He served with the army in Egypt! Alexandria, to be precise. Which is where she comes from. Who knows what goes on in the minds of women there? They're not like white women, you know! But she's definitely moved up a bit now. She's the mistress of a cabinet minister, Member of Parliament for a Manchester constituency, where all the trouble is over the cotton at the moment. She's not got time for the likes of a soldier who's only on the bottom rung of the diplomatic ladder. I dare say he was less keen in taking "no" for an answer, and she didn't want him interfering in her new affair and upsetting Mr Ryerson with tales of her past.'

'Any evidence of that?' Pitt asked. He was angry, and he wanted to prove Talbot prejudiced and inaccurate, but he could not dislike him totally – in fact he could not seriously dislike him at all. The man was faced with a task in which he could not satisfy his superiors and still keep any kind of honour. Neither would he keep the confidence of the men he commanded, and with whom he would have to work after this affair was over.

'Of course I haven't!' Talbot responded. 'But I'll lay you a pound to a penny that if Special Branch, or someone like them, doesn't charge in and prevent me, I will have in a day or two. The crime's only four hours old!'

Pitt knew he was being unfair.

'How did you identify him?' he asked.

'He had cards on him,' Talbot said simply, sitting back upright again. 'She was going to dispose of the body. She hadn't even bothered to remove them.'

'Is that what she said?'

'For God's sake, man!' Talbot exploded. 'She was caught in the garden with his body in a wheelbarrow! What else was she going to do with him? She wasn't taking him to a doctor! He was already dead. She didn't call the police, as an innocent woman would have done, she fetched the gardener's barrow, heaved him into it, and started to wheel him away.'

'To go where?' Pitt asked, trying to imagine what had been in the woman's mind, apart from hysteria.

Talbot looked very slightly discomfited. 'She won't say,' he replied.

Pitt raised his eyebrows very slightly. 'And what about Mr Ryerson?'

'I haven't asked!' Talbot snapped. 'And I don't want to know! He wasn't on the scene when the police got there. He arrived a few moments afterwards.'

'What?' Pitt said incredulously.

Talbot coloured. 'He arrived a few moments afterwards,' he repeated stubbornly.

'He just happened to be passing at three in the morning, saw the light of the constable's bull's-eye shining on a woman with a corpse in a wheelbarrow, so he stopped to see if he could help?' Pitt said with heavy sarcasm. 'He did arrive in a carriage, from the street, I assume? He didn't by any chance come out of the house – in his nightshirt!'

'No, he did not!' Talbot retorted hotly, his thin face flushing. 'He was fully dressed, and he walked over from the direction of the street.'

'Where his carriage was waiting, no doubt?'

'He said he came by hansom,' Talbot answered.

'Intending to call on the lady, only to find her conspicuously unprepared!' Pitt observed waspishly. 'And you believe him?'

'What choice do I have?' Talbot raised his voice for the first time, his desperation ragged through his rapidly slipping composure. 'It's idiotic, I know that! Of course he was there. He was actually coming from the mews, where I imagine he'd gone to harness up a horse and hitch it to a trap, or whatever she has, to take the body somewhere and get rid of it. They're only a stone's throw from Hyde Park. That would do. It would be found, of course, but there would be nothing to connect it with either of them. But we got there too soon. We didn't see him with her, and she isn't saying anything.'

'And you don't ask him because you don't want to know,' Pitt finished for him.

'Something like that,' Talbot admitted, his eyes hot and wretched. 'But if you want to, then Special Branch is very welcome. Have it! Have it all! Go and ask him. He lives in Paulton Square, Chelsea. I don't know the number, but you can ask. There can't be many cabinet ministers there.'

'I'll see the Egyptian woman first. What is her name?'

'Ayesha Zakhari,' Talbot replied. 'But you can't see her. That's my orders from the top, and Special Branch or not, I'm not letting you in. She hasn't implicated Mr Ryerson so you've no brief here. If her Embassy says anything it'll be a matter for the Foreign Office, or the Lord Chancellor, or whoever. But so far they haven't. She's just an ordinary woman arrested for the murder of an old lover, and there's no reasonable doubt that she did it. That's how it is, sir – and that's how it's staying, as far as I'm concerned. If you want to make it different, you'll have to do it somewhere else, 'cos you're not doing it here.'

139

Pitt pushed his hands into his trouser pockets, finding a small piece of string, half a dozen coins, a bull's-eye sweet wrapped in paper, two odd lumps of sealing wax, a penknife and three safety pins. In the other were a notebook, a stub end of pencil and two handkerchiefs. It flicked through his mind that that was too much.

Talbot stared at him. For the first time Pitt saw in his face that he was frightened. He had cause to be. If he were wrong, either for Ryerson or against him, not a matter of fact but of judgement, he would be ruined. He would take the blame, possibly for others' mistakes, men of greater power and with more to lose.

'So Mr Ryerson is at home?' Pitt asked.

'As far as I know,' Talbot said. 'He certainly isn't here. We asked him if he could help us, and he said he couldn't. He said he thought Miss Zakhari was innocent. He didn't believe she would have killed anyone, unless they were threatening her life, in which case it wouldn't be a crime.' He shrugged. 'I could have written it all down without bothering to ask him. He said the only thing he could – he doesn't know anything about it, he only just arrived – to protect her honour, and all that. Decent men don't say a woman's a whore, even if she is and we all know it. And as I said, she didn't deny the gun was hers. We asked the manservant she has, and he admitted it as well. He kept it clean and oiled, and so on.'

'Why did she have a gun?'

Talbot spread his hands. 'God knows! She did, that's all that matters. Look, sir – Constable Cotter found her in the garden with the murdered body of an old lover of hers, stuck in a wheelbarrow. What more do you want of us?'

'Nothing,' Pitt conceded. 'Thank you for your patience, Inspector Talbot. If there's anything further I'll come back.' He hesitated a moment, then smiled. 'Good luck.'

Talbot rolled his eyes, but his expression softened for a moment. 'Thank you,' he said with a touch of sarcasm. 'I wish I could walk away from it so easily!'

Pitt grinned, and went to the door with a feeling of overwhelming relief. Talbot, poor man, was welcome to what was almost certainly no more than a domestic tragedy after all, cabinet minister notwithstanding.

All the same, he decided before going back to report to Narraway that he would walk past Eden Lodge and look at it. Connaught Square was less than ten minutes away and it was now a very pleasant early morning. More deliverymen were out and the clip of horses' hoofs was sharp in the air. In the areaway of one large house a between-stairs maid of about fourteen was whacking a red and blue rug with enthusiasm and sending a fine cloud of dust up into the sunlight. Pitt wondered if it was just exuberance, or if the rug stood in for someone she disliked.

He crossed the road, cobbles still gleaming in the dew, and threw a penny to one of the small boys who swept away the manure when the need arose. It was too early for him to have much to do yet, and he leaned on his broom, his flat cap a couple of sizes too big for him, and resting on his ears.

'Ta, mister!' he called back with a grin.

Eden Lodge was an imposing house facing the open space of Connaught Square, and with a further wide view of St George's Burial Ground behind it, beyond the mews. It might be interesting to find out whether Miss Zakhari owned the house or rented it, and if the latter, from whom? Or possibly they had not bothered to be so discreet, and it was simply owned by Ryerson in the first place.

But of more importance now was to see the garden where she had been found with the corpse. For that it would be necessary to walk the short distance to the end of the block and round to the back.

There was a constable on duty in the mews and Pitt identified himself before being permitted to go through the gate beside the stables and into the leafy, damp, early autumn garden. He kept to the path, although there was little to mask or spoil in the way of evidence. The wooden wheelbarrow was still there, smears of blood down the right side, from where the person pushing it would have stood, and a dark pool, almost congealed, in the bottom. The dead man must have been laid across it with his head on that side and his legs over the other.

Pitt bent and looked more closely at the ground. The wheel was sunk almost an inch deep in the loam, witnessing the weight of the load. The rut it had caused was deep for about three yards, and from that point there were tracks where it had come, empty, been turned around and loaded. He straightened up and walked the few yards.

142

Faint scuff marks, indistinct, showed where feet had stood and swivelled, but it was impossible even to tell how many, let alone whether they were a man or woman's, or both. The earth was scattered with fallen leaves and twigs and occasional small pebbles, leaving only rough traces of passage.

However, when Pitt looked more closely the rusty mark of blood was clear enough. This was where Lovat had been when he fell.

He stared around him. He was about five yards into the garden, between laurel and rhododendron bushes, and in the dappled shade of birches towering a great deal higher. He was completely concealed from the mews, and obviously from the street, by the bulk of the house itself. He was a good five yards from the stone wall that concealed the back entrance to the scullery and areaway, and ahead of him across a strip of open lawn edged by flowers was a french door to the main part of the house.

What on earth had Edwin Lovat been doing here? It seemed unlikely he had arrived through the mews and was intending coming in this way, unless by prior arrangement, and she had been waiting for him inside the french doors. If she had not wished to see him, it would have been simple enough not to have answered. Servants could have dismissed him, and thrown him out if necessary.

If he were indeed arriving, it looked unpleasantly as if she had lured him here deliberately, with the intent of killing him, since she was in the garden with a loaded gun.

Or else he had been leaving, they had quarrelled and

she had followed him out, again with the gun.

When had Ryerson really arrived? Before the shooting, or after? Had she lifted the dead man into the wheelbarrow by herself? It would be interesting to find out his size and weight, and hers. If she had lifted him, then there would be blood, and perhaps earth, on her white dress. These were questions he needed to ask Talbot, or perhaps the constable who had actually been first on the scene.

He turned and walked back through the gate to the mews and found the constable standing fidgeting from one foot to the other in boredom. He turned as he heard the gate catch.

'Were you on duty here last night?' Pitt asked. The man looked tired enough to have been up many hours.

'Yes, sir.'

'Did you see the arrest of Miss Zakhari?'

'Yes, sir.' His voice lifted a little with the beginning of interest.

'Can you describe her for me?'

He looked startled for a moment, then his face puckered in concentration. 'She is quite tall, sir, but very slender, like. And foreign, o'course, very foreign, like. She was . . . well, she moved very graceful, more than most ladies – not that they aren't—'

'It's all right, Constable,' Pitt answered him. 'I need honesty, not tact. What about the dead man, how large was he?'

'Oh, bit bigger than most, sir, broad in the chest, like. Difficult ter say 'ow tall 'cos I never saw 'im standin' up, but I reckon a bit taller'n me, but not as tall as you.'

'Did the mortuary wagon take him away?'

'Yes, sir.'

'How many men to carry him?'

'Two, sir.' His face filled with understanding. 'You thinkin' as she couldn't 'ave put 'im in that barrer by 'erself?'

'Yes, I was.' Pitt tightened his lips. 'But it might be wiser not to express that opinion to others, at least for the time being. She was wearing white, so I'm told. Is that correct?'

'Yes, sir. Very sort o' close fittin' dress, it were, not exactly like most ladies wear, least wot I've seen. Very beautiful . . .' He coloured faintly, considering the propriety of saying that a murderess was beautiful, and a foreign one at that. But he refused to be cowed. 'Sort o' more natural, like,' he went on. 'No . . .' he put one hand on his other shoulder, 'no puffs up 'ere. More wot a woman's really shaped like.'

Pitt hid a smile. 'I see. And was it stained with mud, or blood, this white dress?'

'Bit o' mud, or more like leaf dirt,' the constable agreed.

'Where?'

'Around the knees, sir. Like she kneeled on the ground.'

'But no blood?'

'No, sir. Not that I saw.' His eyes widened. 'You're sayin' as she didn't put 'im in that barrer 'erself!'

'No, Constable, I think you are. But I'd be very obliged if you did not repeat that, unless you are asked to do so in a situation where not doing so would require you to lie. Don't lie to anyone.'

'No, sir! I'll 'ope as I'm not asked.'

'Yes, that would definitely be the best,' Pitt agreed fervently. 'Thank you, Constable. What is your name?'

'Cotter, sir.'

'Is the manservant still in the house?'

'Yes, sir. No one's come out since they took 'er away.'

'Then I shall go and speak to him. Do you know his name?'

'No, sir. Foreign-looking person.'

Pitt thanked him again and walked the short distance to the back door. He knocked firmly and waited several minutes before it was opened by a dark-skinned man dressed in pale, stone-coloured robes. Most of his head was covered with a turban. His beard was turning grey. His eyes were almost black.

'Yes, sir?' he said guardedly.

'Good morning,' Pitt replied. 'Are you Miss Zakhari's manservant?'

'Yes, sir. But Miss Zakhari is not at home.' It was said with finality, as if that were the end of any possible discussion. He was obviously preparing to close the door.

'I am aware of that!' Pitt said sharply. 'What is your name?'

'Tariq el Abd, sir,' the man replied.

Pitt produced his card again and held it out, assuming that el Abd could read English. 'I am from Special Branch. I believe the police have already spoken to you, but I need to ask you a few further questions.'

'Oh, I see.' He pulled the door wider open and reluctantly permitted Pitt to go through the scullery and up a step into a warm and exotically fragrant kitchen. There was no one else there. Presumably el Abd did such cooking as was required, and other household staff came in daily to do the laundry and cleaning.

'Would you like some coffee, sir?' el Abd enquired graciously, as if the kitchen were his. His voice was low and he spoke almost without accent.

'Thank you.' Pitt accepted more out of curiosity than a desire for more coffee. There was a smell of spices in the air, and strange-shaped loaves of bread cooling on a rack near the further window. Unfamiliar fruit lay rich and burnished in a bowl on the table.

El Abd took only a few moments to bring the coffee to the desired temperature again and bring a tiny cup of it over to present to Pitt, offering him a seat and enquiring after his comfort. He was a lean man who moved with a silent grace, which made his age difficult to estimate, but the weathered skin of his hands made Pitt guess him to be well over forty, perhaps closer to fifty.

Pitt thanked him for the coffee and sipped it. It was so strong as to be almost a syrup, and he did not care for it much, but he kept all expression from his face except polite enquiry.

'What happened here last night?' he asked.

El Abd remained standing, so Pitt was forced to look up at him.

'I do not know, sir,' he replied. 'Something awakened

me, and I arose to see if Miss Zakhari had called, but I could not find her anywhere in the house.' He hesitated.

'Yes?' Pitt prompted him.

El Abd looked down at the floor. 'I went to the window and I saw nothing to the front, so I went to the back, and I saw movement through the bushes, the ones with the flat, shining leaves. I waited a few moments, but there was no more sound, and I knew of no reason to suppose there was anything wrong. I thought then that perhaps it was only the sound of the door that had wakened me.'

'What did you do then?'

He lifted his shoulders very slightly. 'I was not required, sir. I went back to my bed. I do not know how long it was until I heard the people speaking, and the police called me downstairs.'

'Did they show you a gun?'

'Yes, sir.'

'And ask you whose it was?'

'Yes, sir. I said it was Miss Zakhari's.' He looked down at the floor. 'I did not know then what it had been used for. But I clean it and oil it, so of course I know it well.'

'Why does Miss Zakhari have a gun?'

'It is not my place to ask such questions, sir.'

'And you don't know?'

'No, sir.'

'I see. But you would know if she had ever fired it before, since you clean it?'

'No, sir, she has not.'

148

'Thank you. Did you know Lieutenant Lovat . . . the dead man?'

'I do not think he has been here before.'

That was not precisely what Pitt had asked, and he was aware of the evasion. Was it deliberate, or simply that the man was speaking a language other than his own?

'Have you seen him before?'

El Abd lowered his eyes. 'I have not seen him at all, sir. It is my understanding that the policeman knew who he was from his clothes, and the things in his pockets.'

So they had not asked el Abd if he had seen Lovat before. That was an omission, but perhaps not one that would make a great deal of difference. He was Miss Zakhari's servant. Now that he knew she was accused of murdering him, he would probably deny knowledge of him anyway.

Pitt finished his coffee and rose to his feet. 'Thank you,' he said, trying to swallow the last of the sweet, sticky liquid and clean his mouth of the taste.

'Sir,' el Abd bowed very slightly, no more than a gesture.

Pitt went out of the back door, thanked Constable Cotter as he passed him, walked away along the mews, round the corner into Connaught Square, and looked for a hansom to take him back to Narraway.

'Well?' Narraway looked up from the papers he was reading. His face was a little pinched, his eyes anxious.

'The police are holding the woman, Ayesha Zakhari,

and completely ignoring Ryerson,' Pitt told him. 'They aren't investigating the murder too closely because they don't want to know the answer.' He walked over and sat down in the chair in front of Narraway's desk.

Narraway breathed in deeply, and then out again. 'And what are the answers?' he asked, his voice quiet and very level. There was a stillness about him as if his attention were so heightened he dared not distract himself by even the slightest action.

Pitt found himself unconsciously copying, refraining from crossing one leg over the other.

'That Ryerson helped her, at least in attempting to dispose of the body,' he replied.

'Indeed . . .' Narraway breathed out slowly, but none of the tension disappeared from him. 'And what evidence told you that?'

'She is a slender woman, at the time wearing a white dress,' Pitt replied. 'The dead man was slightly over average height and weight. It took two mortuary attendants to lift him from the barrow into the wagon, although of course they may have been more careful with him than whoever was trying to dispose of him.'

Narraway nodded, his lips tight.

'But her white dress was not stained with mud or blood,' Pitt went on. 'Only a little leaf mould where she had kneeled on the ground, possibly beside him where he lay.'

'I see.' Narraway's voice was tight, almost expressionless. 'And Ryerson?'

150

'I didn't ask,' Pitt said. 'The constable was quite aware of why I enquired, and of the obvious conclusions. Do you want me to go back and ask him? I can do perfectly easily, but it will then—'

'I can work that out for myself, Pitt!' Narraway snapped. 'No. I do not want you to do that . . . at least not yet.' His eyes flickered for a moment, then he looked over at the far wall. 'We'll see what happens.'

Pitt sat still, aware of a curious, unfinished air in the room, as if elusive but powerful things were just beyond the edge of perception. Narraway had left something unsaid. Did it matter? Or was it just an accumulation of knowledge gathered over the years, a feeling of unease rather than a thought?

Narraway hesitated also, then the moment passed and he looked up at Pitt again. 'Well, go on!' he said, but with less asperity than before. 'You've told me what you saw and what the constable reported. We'll save Ryerson from himself, if we can. The next move is up to the police. Go home and have breakfast. I might want you later.'

Pitt stood up, still looking at Narraway, who stared back at him, his eyes bright, almost blank of emotion, but it was deliberately concealed, not absent. Pitt was as certain of that as he was of the charge in the room like electricity in the air on a sultry day.

'Yes, sir,' he said quietly, and with Narraway still looking at him, he went out of the door.

When he got home it was late morning. His children,

Jemima and Daniel, were at school, and Charlotte and
the maid, Gracie, were in the kitchen. He heard their
laughter as soon as he opened the front door. He smiled
to himself as he bent and took off his boots. The sounds
washed around him like a balm – women's voices, the
clatter of pans, a kettle whistling shrilly. The house was
warm from the kitchen stove and there was an odour of
freshly laundered cotton, still a little damp, clean wood
from the scrubbed floor, and baking bread.

A marmalade-striped cat came out of the kitchen
doorway and stretched luxuriously, then trotted towards
him, tail up in a question mark.

'Hello, Archie,' he said softly, stroking it as it swivelled
round under his hand, pressing against him and purring.
'I suppose you want half my breakfast?' he went on.
'Well, come on then.' He stood up and walked silently
down to the doorway, the cat following.

In the kitchen Charlotte was tipping bread out of its tin
on to a rack to cool, and Gracie, still small and thin
although she was now well over twenty, was putting clean
blue and white china away on the Welsh dresser.

Sensing his presence rather than seeing him, Charlotte
turned round, questions in her face.

'Breakfast,' he replied with a smile.

Gracie did not ask anything. She was outspoken
enough once she was involved. She did not regard that as
impertinence, rather the role of helping and looking after
him, which she had taken upon herself almost from the
time she had arrived in the household, aged thirteen, half

starved and with all her clothes too big for her. Her hair had been scraped back off her bright little face, and although then she could neither read nor write, she had a wit as sharp as any.

Now she was far more mature, and considered herself to be an invaluable employee of the cleverest detective in England, or anywhere else, a position she would not have exchanged for one in service to the Queen herself.

'It's not the Inner Circle again, is it?' Charlotte said with an edge of fear in her voice.

Gracie stood frozen, the dishes in her hands. No one had forgotten that dreadful, secret organisation that had cost Pitt his career in the Metropolitan Police, and very nearly his life also.

'No,' Pitt said immediately and with certainty. 'It's a simple domestic murder . . .' He saw the disbelief in her face. 'Almost certainly committed by a woman who is the mistress of a senior government minister,' he added. 'Equally certainly he was there, if not at the time, then immediately afterwards, and helped her attempt to get rid of the body.'

'Oh!' she said with instant perception. 'I see. But they didn't get away with it?'

'No.' He sat down on one of the straight-backed wooden chairs and stretched out his legs. 'The alarm was raised by someone who heard the shots and the police arrived in time to catch her in the back garden with the corpse in a wheelbarrow.'

She stared at him in a moment's disbelief, then saw

153

from his eyes that he was not joking.

'Must be a bleedin' idjut!' Gracie said candidly. 'I 'ope 'e in't in charge o' summink wot matters in the gov'ment, or we'll all be in the muck!'

'Yes,' Pitt agreed with feeling. The cat leaped up on to his knee and he stroked it absently, fingers gentle in the deep fur. 'I'm afraid we will.'

Gracie sighed and started to sort out the dishes he would need for breakfast, and to make him a cup of tea first. Charlotte went to the stove to begin cooking, her face eloquent of the trouble she could foresee.